To WAZ
(GO Team!)

*"...But always there is that Eternal Voice,
forever whispering within our ear;
that thing which causes the eternal quest,
that thing which forever sings and sings."*

— Ernest Holmes

Praise for Maggie Vaults Over the Moon ...

"That one in a thousand books you'll carry with you forever!"
--Margaret Wheatley, 16, Florida

"Girls who play sports and the coaches and families who support them will thoroughly enjoy this warm, uplifting story."
--Christine Brennan, *USA TODAY*

"An inspirational pick for young adult fiction collections."
--*MIDWEST BOOK REVIEW*"

"A fine YA novel about perseverance in sports and in life."
--*KIRKUS REVIEWS*

"The positive influence this book can have on young athletes is invaluable."
--Erica (Bartolina) Fraley, US Olympian, Coach of Champions

"An amazing account of heartbreak, struggle, and ultimately success, Maggie inspires all of us to triumph!"
--Mark and Amanda Hollis, US Champion and School Teacher

"I myself experienced loss when I was a young girl. Sports were my outlet and helped me through some of the hardest times of my life. This book captured me cover to cover. I highly recommend it."
--Becky Holliday, US Olympian

"Celebrates the courage to turn tragedy and loss into something positive, and how the determination to master a sport can heal."
--*VAULTER MAGAZINE*

"I enthusiastically recommend it!"
--**Barbara Gruener, National School of Character Coach**

"One of the most pure and wholesome young adult books I've ever read, appropriate for 4th grade and up."
--**Shannon Clark, Girls Gone Sporty Ambassador**

"I loved the book and wish I had written it."
--**Kimbrook Tennal, High School Coach**

"I highly recommend it for all teens, especially those seeking direction during the storm and stress of adolescence."
--**Timothy M. Tays, Ph.D., Clinical Psychologist**

"A well-written tale of epic courage."
--**Kim Ring, Middle School Teacher**

"*Maggie* has a tragedy without being gruesome, a love story that is innocent, and sports competitors that exhibit true sportsmanship. Truly refreshing. The world needs more Maggies!"
--**Jolene Frook, Sports Mom**

"A beautiful story of triumph through adversity."
--**Bill Vogrin, *COLORADO SPRINGS GAZETTE***

"Heartwarming and realistic, this book is a winner."
--**Nancy Julien Kopp, *CHICKEN SOUP & GUIDEPOST***

"Even non-athletes will find this book captivating."
--**Mark (Doc) Breault, Tailwind Pole Vault Club**

"Will translate to anyone who allows themselves to be young at heart."
--**John Rinkenbaugh, TV Producer, Former Kansas Boy**

"A magical story written through the eyes of a teen."
--**Mark Miranda, Sports Dad**

"I've probably read it more than twenty times!"
--*Taylor Millsap, 14, Illinois*

Maggie Vaults Over the Moon

By
GRANT OVERSTAKE

ISBN: 1478296879
ISBN 13: 9781478296874
Library of Congress Control Number: 2012913473
CreateSpace, North Charleston, South Carolina

CHAPTER 1

Here in Grain Valley Township, we don't have paid professional fire-fighters or emergency rescue crews to rescue us. We rescue ourselves.

My dad has been a volunteer fireman since he was eighteen. Carries his emergency radio everywhere, fastened to the belt of his jeans. At night, his radio sits on his nightstand. When it goes off, he springs out of bed no matter what time it is. It doesn't happen every night or even every week, but it happens often enough for me to worry about him. Which is too often, I'd say.

Like the time Dad and the other volunteers got called out of our little church on Sunday morning. The preacher was leading us in the Lord's Prayer when beeping radios went off all over the sanctuary. We said an extra prayer for all the men who up and bolted for the door that day.

Being a volunteer firefighter seems exciting and I've thought about becoming one myself next year, when I turn eighteen. I know I could do what they do, if given a chance. But being a fireman is strictly a guy thing around here.

It would be exciting to be one, but at the same time, it's dangerous and stressful to go out on emergency calls. For one thing, you never know what kind of accident you'll be responding to, or how bad someone is hurt. And for another thing, since everybody knows everybody else around here, there's a good chance that whoever desperately needs your help will be somebody you know.

Now it was just after eleven o'clock on Friday night, June third, almost a year ago, when Dad and Mom and I heard the radio alarm. I was in the bathroom washing my face and getting ready for bed when Dad rushed from the bedroom toward the kitchen and dashed out the back door to his pickup. The radio screeched, "Two-car crash, cars on fire, three miles east of Grain Valley on 39 Highway," as the screen door slammed. The engine roared and tires spun on the gravel as he sped away into the night.

When the alarm goes out, whoever gets to the firehouse first opens the big metal doors, and starts one or both of the fire trucks, depending on how serious the call is. The other men show up within two or three minutes, pulling their coats and gloves on, on the run.

Mom came out from the bedroom in her robe, fussing with her short, graying hair. With the radio gone, the house was quiet. We heard sirens wailing through the screen door. Both trucks were on the roll. "Sounds like a bad one, Maggie," Mom said, brow furrowed. "Have you heard from Alex and Caleb?"

"Not since before supper," I said.

"Why don't you call. See where they're at."

I hit the speed dial on my cell phone for my brother, Alex, but it went straight to voice mail. "Hey, there's a wreck on the highway, and Mom wants to hear from you guys." Then I speed-dialed my boyfriend, Caleb, but got the same result, voice mail.

After that we just sat there at the kitchen table, as the clock ticked and the refrigerator hummed and the crickets chirped. We had no way of knowing what Dad would find out there on the highway. We sat there for twenty minutes or so, but nobody called.

Finally Mom said, "Well, maybe they're still at the movies."

I nodded. "Or maybe they're just out of range."

We get lousy cell phone coverage here in rural Kansas.

They say there's a special bond between a sister and her brother, that they always know when the other one is in serious trouble or something's gone terribly wrong. Since I didn't have any bad feelings, I thought Alex and Caleb were fine. I expected them to roll in any minute, laughing and joking around, heading straight for the fridge to eat us out of house and home. Whoever it was out there in that awful car wreck, I was sure it wasn't them.

I couldn't have been more wrong.

CHAPTER 2

The doorbell never rings at our house unless a total stranger comes to call. People who know us always come to the back door that leads into the kitchen.

We were still sitting at the kitchen table when the doorbell rang. We both jumped half out of our skins. The doorbell rang again as I was rushing down the hallway that led to the living room, and a third time just as I yanked the front door open and clicked the porch light on. I saw Reverend Stark and his son, Scott, standing in the yellow light that keeps bugs away. One of the cats was weaving around Scott's legs. Mom stood behind me in the doorway, I felt her hand on my back. I glanced back at her. Her eyes were wide.

My hands felt numb as I fumbled with the latch on the screen door. The door groaned open and hissed closed as the pastor and his son came inside. I flipped the second switch on the wall, turning on the living room light. The four of us just stood there for a long moment.

Reverend Stark cleared his throat and gestured toward the sofa. "Please, Mrs. Steele, Maggie," he said. "I'm afraid I have some very bad news."

Mom and I sat next to each other on the sofa, both of her hands in both of mine. The pastor knelt down in front of us and put his fat hand and short pudgy fingers on top of ours. He wore a gold pinky ring with a dull square ruby. His cologne was sickeningly sweet. He was wearing the same black suit and red tie he wore to funerals. It had grown tight in the past few years.

In the same preacher voice he used on Sunday, he said, "There was a bad wreck. The truck your son, Alex, and the Miller boy, Caleb, were in was hit by another car. All three of them died. Them boys have gone to be with Jesus, which is a good thing. But I'm sorry."

A shock buzzed through my body, numbing my legs and feet. Mom was bone white, grey eyes staring, frozen.

The pastor's fat fingers were still patting our hands. I jerked mine away and glared at him.

"No. That can't be right," I said. "Alex and Caleb went to the movies. They'll be home any minute."

Scott shifted uneasily. He caught my glance and looked away.

The pastor began to recite scripture from memory. "The Lord is my shepherd, I shall not want. He makes me lie down in green pastures..." His voice sounded hollow, like he was talking in an empty grain bin.

Suddenly my stomach lurched. I couldn't help it. I hurled, on the rug, on the sofa; on the preacher's pants and shoes. The vomit tasted bitter and burned my nose.

"Jeezus!" Scott said.

"Son! Go to the car! Now!"

To this day, I think I saw a smirk on Scott's face as he went out the door.

Mom went to the kitchen and came back with a roll of paper towels and the trash can. I was a mess, and felt like I wasn't done.

"Go to the bathroom," Mom said. "Put your clothes in the sink and get in the shower. I'll bring you something to sleep in."

I remember taking a hot shower; rinsing my long brown hair for a long time. I wiped the steam off the mirror. Blue eyes looked back at me. My face was sad and pale.

When I got into bed, my throat was still burning from the you-know-what. When I woke up, my first thought was that I'd had a terrible nightmare about my brother and my boyfriend.

CHAPTER 3

It was the doorbell that woke me. I heard the front door squeak open and Dad talking in a low voice. A moment later, there was a soft knock at my door. Dad leaned inside. He looked terrible.

"Maggie?" he said softly. "You awake, honey?" He'd never called me honey before.

The knot in my stomach reminded me of last night: my nightmare.

"Is Alex home yet?" I asked.

Dad shook his head. "No, he isn't."

"I'll be out in a minute," I said. I closed my eyes, wishing that the morning hadn't come. I felt as if my room were spinning. I was over-taken by nausea and felt as if I would hurl again, but there was nothing left. And that's all I want to say about that.

The doorbell rang a lot that morning. Church ladies brought food and hugged me close and said dear-dear and patted me on the back. My grandma sat next to me on the couch. She braided my hair and rubbed my back, and we held hands. We wiped our eyes and nodded as people came and went. Mostly I just sat there feeling numb, allowing myself to get hugged.

I smelled like old women's perfume. It reminded me of Rev. Stark's stinky cologne and about Scott being there to see me puke. I felt upset about ralphing in front of Scott. I'd never liked him anyway, not since he tried to kiss me after the Christmas pageant, when he was Joseph and I was Mary, when we were in the fifth grade. And there'd been other stuff. When I'd told Alex that Scott had tried to kiss me, he pushed him down the church basement stairs. We thought we'd be in big trouble but Scott never told. The Starks had moved into the church parsonage that spring. At first we'd been excited they had a boy our same age. Too bad he turned out to be a jerk.

I was proud of Alex that day. But we'd started some big trouble with Scott Stark. The kind of trouble that doesn't go away.

CHAPTER 4

Our kitchen looked like the church kitchen before a Fifth Sunday dinner. Covered dishes. Deviled eggs. Fried chicken in aluminum foil. Gallon jugs of sweet iced tea. In other words, funeral food.

"I'm sure they mean well," Mom said, looking at the food stacked everyplace. There were fifteen bags of chips on the kitchen counter, an offering to a Cheetos god. At the same time, the same thing was happening over at the Millers' house, two miles away. I was sure that my best friend, Betsy, Caleb's sister, and her parents were probably having just as many people come to pay their respects and just as much church food piled up in their kitchen, as untouched as ours.

Betsy is my best friend, but for some reason we didn't speak for a few days after the accident. We finally saw each other before the shared funeral, which was held the following Saturday morning in the high school gym. We hugged each other in the science room where they put our families. I held her tight. We had a lot to cry about.

Our brothers had been killed at the same time. But even more than that, my brother was Betsy's boyfriend. They were a serious couple. And Caleb was my boyfriend. And now they were just...gone.

They'd rolled in the big piano from the auditorium. The lady who accompanies the choir played as the families walked into the gym, the Millers and the Steeles.

The people standing in the back were asked to please find a seat. The people sitting in the chairs set up on the basketball court moved in to the center to make room for everybody, but the gym was standing-room only. Betsy and I sat next to each other in folding chairs in the front row, right in front of the closed caskets. There were boxes of tissues under every seat. I didn't think I had any more tears left in me, but I did. We all did.

Our principal, Dr. Taylor, blew his nose and wiped his eyes and said, "This is a very sad day for all of us here at Grain Valley. I'm sure the families here on the front row are comforted by your being here." He hesitated, like he wanted to say more. He looked at the framed gradu-ation pictures of our boys on top of the caskets, raised his hand like he wanted to comment on their looks or kindness or athleticism or popu-larity, but couldn't. He shook his head and looked at Betsy and me. I knew he was just trying to say, "We're all so sorry," but instead he just shook his head again, and sat down.

Then Rev. Stark came to the podium. I hadn't seen him since he delivered the bad news. We sat through his *looong* sermon. I didn't hear most of it. He did ask everyone to repent of their sins and turn to Jesus, which seemed strange. I looked at Dad sitting next to Mom. Tears wetted his tanned face. But his jaw was clenched, and so were his fists.

I heard a lot of people blowing their noses during the closing prayer. They had the families go out the side door into the glaring summer sun. We stood there as twelve guys from the Grain Valley lettermen's club, wearing their letter jackets, carried our brothers to their respective hearses. It was unreal to watch.

Betsy and her family got in a black limousine. Mom and Dad and Grandma and I got in ours. The Millers followed Caleb's hearse toward the Grain Valley town cemetery, where they laid him to rest with rela-tives who were already buried there. We followed Alex's hearse along a county road to the old graveyard next to our church. My grandpa was buried there alongside a lot of my ancestors.

The gusty south wind whipped the green funeral tent. It rattled the chains against the metal tent poles. The lettermen carried Alex from the hearse and put him on the stand hovering over a deep, dark hole. I wanted so desperately to open the casket and get him out of there. The guys unfolded a gold Grain Valley High School flag and laid it on the top of the casket, but the wind blew it off. One of them picked it up and put it back on again, and they all held it in place for the rest of the ceremony.

It took quite a while for all of the people to drive from the high school to the church parking lot, and then walk across the graveyard. There were people all around, inside and outside the tent. But the ser-vice took no time at all.

Afterward, Rev. Stark shook our hands. "Your brother's in a better place," he said to me.

My hair whipped into my eyes, and I had to hold it back to look at him.

"Thank you," I said, instantly regretting it.

They didn't lower the casket while we were there. I didn't see Alex disappear into the hole, dug deep in the Kansas soil. But a few days later we went back to the graveyard, all of us, Mom and Dad and Grandma and me, to see Alex's headstone. It was made of gray marble, flecked with gold. The GV high school logo was etched on it, just like on the letter jacket he wore.

Mom, who hadn't said more than a dozen words since the accident, asked Dad something that I couldn't hear because of the wind. The black dirt was still piled up high.

"The dirt will sink down, and the grass will sprout here in a few days," he answered her.

We stood looking at Alex's headstone for a long while. Grandma finally said, "Well, it looks nice, don't you think?"

I nodded. I found out later she'd paid for it herself, but I don't know how much it cost.

Before we left, Grandma walked the short distance to Grandpa's grave, knelt by his marker, and said, "You take good care of our boy now."

We walked back to the car. Nobody said anything.

There wasn't anything left to say.

CHAPTER 5

We drove back to the farm, which can be seen from a mile away on the flat Kansas prairie. It's the same farm that my great-great-grandparents homesteaded, but it's different now in a thousand ways. In the past, the Steeles ran a big cattle operation. There were cows grazing all over the place. Plus, we had three thousand acres back then.

When my dad was a boy growing up here, he and Grandpa rode horses to round up cows and mend barbed-wire fences. They also had several farmhands, or helpers, who rode horses. And early in the last century, they used horses and mules to plow the cropland. Our old barn stands as a reminder of the old days. It's really huge, four times as big as the farmhouse. It had to be because of the way they farmed and worked cattle. The barn was where they kept everything. The equipment and the horses stayed on the ground floor. Above that is the giant hayloft, which is my favorite place on the entire farm. It was Alex's favorite place, too.

We got into the loft by the wood-slat ladder, through the square opening in the floor of the loft. Looking up, one can see all the way to the roof of the barn, which is incredibly high. I used to be scared to climb up there, when I was five or six. Now it's no big deal. Even the cats do it.

The hayloft itself is ginormous. There's plenty of room to run around, as big as half a gym. In fact, there's a basketball backboard mounted up there on the far wall. Alex and I used to shoot baskets up here. There's even a free-throw line painted on the old wooden floor. Dad and Alex had used a tape measure to put it down exactly right. The white paint has faded, but if you look closely, you can still see little cat prints where one of the cats walked across the line when the paint was wet. I thought it was funny, but Alex sure didn't.

The backboard was pretty hard to see in the shadowy loft, which was why Dad put the lights in, running the electricity from the house. Alex helped dig the trench across the yard. Now, when I flip the switch, the loft is filled with light from a half-dozen bulbs mounted on the beams.

The best things about the hayloft are the climbing ropes. Alex and I called them the Tarzan Swings. The ropes have been hanging from the rafters, as high as I could see, since I was old enough to climb up there. They're real climbing ropes. My dad bought three of them at the auction after the old K–8 school was shut down due to consolidation. They auctioned the desks and chalkboards and everything, including the gym equipment. I don't know how Dad ever got the ropes hung up there so high, but he did. The other rope is hanging from a tree, down at the creek.

The ropes were still hanging there when I climbed up after returning from Alex's grave. I walked over to one and grabbed it like I'd done a thousand times before, remembering what the ropes had meant to Alex and me. We'd learned to climb there, daring each other to go higher and higher until one day he made it all the way to the top, pounding the roof of the barn with his fist. He let out a yell even Tarzan would have been proud of.

Alex was amazing. He was always the strongest boy in his class, the fastest boy in the fourth, fifth, and sixth grade. I couldn't keep up with him but I tried—oh, how I tried.

We'd swung on these ropes until we got blisters. We were Tarzan and Jane, swinging through the jungle. We were pirates on a ship at sea. After Dad put ladders on the walls on each side of the barn, we'd swing clear across the floor to the ladder on the other side. I can remember how terrified I was at first, but of course Alex took to rope-swinging fearlessly. He swung from the very top rung of the ladder the first time he tried it. We must have swung across that jungle a thousand times, and challenged Captain Blackbeard a thousand more.

I smiled thinking about the time Alex decided that what we really needed was a pile of straw to land in, so we made one. He'd swung from the top rung, flown completely over the straw pile, and landed with a terrible thud on the hardwood floor, missing the straw by a good ten feet.

"Are you all right?" I'd asked.

"Call 9-1-1!" he wheezed, breathlessly.

I burst out laughing. If I'd had a camera, we would've won $10,000 on *America's Funniest Home Videos.*

"You will tell no one about this!" he said.

"Oh, sure!" I giggled. "I'll never tell!" And I'd kept that promise. Even though Alex had an egg-sized bump on the back of his head and scrapes on both elbows, that didn't stop him from trying again, as soon as he was able to get back up. I can still see Alex grabbing that rope and stomping to the ladder, his jaw clenched with determination.

"Watch this!" he'd said. He swung across the floor like before, but just as the rope reached its height on the other side, he swung his legs over his head and let go, turning a beautiful back flip as he fell into the straw. It was the most awesome thing I'd ever seen. I could see him now, shouting, "TA-DA!" and raising his hands in a cloud of falling straw.

All this had happened when Alex was only ten. But it was clear even then that he was more than just an athlete. He was special. But now he was dead. And I was in this hayloft, alone.

CHAPTER 6

On the morning after we went to visit Alex's grave, I went out to the old barn as usual, unlatched the door hook, and went inside. I come here every morning before breakfast to feed the cats. Depending on the time of year, there might be a dozen cats hanging around our farm, and twenty or thirty kittens. Every few months, one of the mama cats will have a litter, which is why we buy cat food in fifty-pound bags at the feed store. We keep it away from the mice in a big metal barrel with a lid held down by a brick, which also keeps the cats from helping themselves. Feeding them is just one my many farm chores, but it isn't really a *chore* chore, because I like it.

The grown-up cats wait for me at the back door of the house every morning. They meow and meow and follow me across the yard to the barn, running ahead of me or weaving around my legs. I open the barn doors and they all rush inside and dash to the food barrel.

This morning I counted fifteen big cats curling around my legs and purring with delight, and if you've ever heard fifteen cats purring, you know it's a pretty wonderful sound. I used an old coffee can to scoop food into three metal bowls we've used since before I was born, and spread them around on the floor. The cats dashed around to find a place to eat, killing their food with violent shakes of their heads, purring and crunching like they hadn't eaten for a week, even though they'd eaten yesterday. That's when I noticed one of the pregnant cats was missing.

I looked around the barn. Old tools and equipment hung on posts. I walked across the barn, thinking I might find the pregnant cat in one of the stalls where plow horses once bedded down. Cracked and crusty harnesses still hung on the far wall. There were teeth marks on the stalls, but the marks are very old because we've never had horses.

I heard a little meow. A new litter of kittens had been born! The mother cat was lying on her side, kneading the straw with her front claws and purring contentedly, eyes closed.

"Hello, mommy cat. Did you have your kittens last night? How many did you have?" I knelt down and counted the little lumps of fur. Two black ones, one white, and two calicos.

"Five new kittens! Congratulations, Momma!"

I pulled one of the calico ones from off its milk and held it up close to my face. "You are a cute little girl, yes you are! If I could name you, I would name you Snuggles because you are so snuggly."

Our farm cats don't get names. Mom says it's better not to name something that will die or be killed or disappear. "There's enough pain in this life," she said. "You don't need to go making friends with farm cats. No need for that nonsense. No need."

The kitten meowed and sucked with its little mouth, wondering where breakfast had gone. It felt new and alive and warm. I put it down in front of the swollen red nipple it had been nursing on. I stroked the mommy cat and rubbed her ears. She purred and leaned her head into my hand for more.

There was something under the mother's back leg. I lifted it and saw a tiny little cat paw. Reaching down, I felt a fuzzy lump. I held the kitten close to my face. There was nothing wrong with it that I could see. It was still warm, but it was dead.

And that did it. I was crying again.

I carried the little kitten out of the barn, across the yard, and through the back door and into the kitchen. Dad was drinking coffee at the table. I just stood there as the screen door slammed shut, not saying a word. Mom stood at the sink, her back to me. She turned around, wiping her hands on her dish towel. When she saw the kitten, she said, "Maggie! Not in the house!"

"Take it outside," Dad said. "I'll get the shovel."

Dad pushed the screen door and went outside. I stayed in the kitchen, holding the kitten. I couldn't stop crying.

"Maggie!" Mom said. "Now!"

"I hate you!" I shouted, and I slammed the door behind me.

I followed Dad outside to the back of the barn and over to our animal graveyard. There are lots of sad memories there. Dad was already digging. He stomped the edge of the shovel with his work boot, slicing the ground. After a minute, he stepped back to make room for me. I laid the nameless kitten in the hole. Dad took a bandanna from his pocket and dangled it in front of me. I blew my nose and handed it back to him. He reached down and lifted the kitten back out of the hole, laid the bandanna on his big hand, and put the tiny kitten on top of it. He wrapped it up tight and returned it to the grave. Then he dropped to his knees, sobbing.

I buried my face in his shirt.

"I'm sure glad I carry two of these," he said, pulling out another bandanna. He took off his glasses and wiped his eyes. He put one arm around me.

"Well, I guess we've had our moment for today, haven't we?"

"I guess so," I sniffed.

"You go on back in the house. I'll take care of this."

"No, that's okay."

Dad took the shovel and put dirt back into the hole until the kitten was all covered over. We walked back to the house together, side by side, and went into the kitchen with its coffee and bacon smells. I sat down to eat scrambled eggs and bacon and buttered toast. Mom poured me a cup of coffee, to which I added lots of sugar.

"Thank you," I said. I was sorry for saying that I hated her.

Mom touched me on the shoulder. I looked at her face. Her eyes were wet. She noticed that I noticed, then turned back to the sink. "You're welcome. Eat now. Your breakfast will get cold."

"Okay," I said.

And that was that.

CHAPTER 7

After breakfast, my stomach was hurting again, so I went to see Grandma. Her house lies at the end of the path from our back door, beyond the garden where we grow our own vegetables. I climbed the wooden steps, walked across the porch, and knocked on her screen door. Her house is like my second home, but I always knock, because it's the polite thing to do.

"Come in! Come in!" she said.

Grandma is round and soft and little and smells like lilacs in the springtime. She hugged me for a long time, then sat me down on the couch and handed me a bowl of fresh-picked peas to shell, while she went to wash her hands after working in the garden.

Her whole house is filled with old furniture. It's like a family museum, and at nearly eighty years old, she's part of that history. As I waited, I looked at old photographs hanging on the walls. One of the photos shows a family standing in front of an old wooden farmhouse. The people in that photo have been looking down on me since I can remember. The grown-ups are grim-faced, and the children seem sad. The father, Great-Grandpa Steele, stands tall and thin in his Sunday suit, holding a hat in his bony hands. I've been told that his eyes were bright blue, like my dad's and mine, but they look almost white in this black-and-white photo. He looks uncomfortable, like he isn't used to being photographed.

Standing next to him is his wife, my great-grandmother, wearing a dark dress over her short, stumpy body. She has a white shawl over her shoulders, held close in front of her. The three children, a boy— my grandfather, Grandma's future husband—and two girls, look at the camera with eyes wide open, like the photographer had told them not to blink. They look so old-fashioned it's hard to imagine they were anything like children are today. One of the girls, Elizabeth, holds an old ragdoll on her lap, clutched in the crook of her elbow. She died a few years ago. The other girl, Rebecca, died of influenza when she was eight years old. Everyone in this photo is buried in the church grave-yard, along with all of the other members of our family who home-steaded our land so long ago.

There have been three different houses on our farm since the beginning. The first farmhouse, the one in the photo, is long gone, torn down in the 1920s. It was replaced by the house where I'm sitting now. The house my family lives in was built for my dad and his new wife, my mom. It's made of brick, and it has white shutters on the windows. It's called a ranch-style, which means it's a long one-story house, with no upstairs.

I looked at another photo on the wall, a much newer one, taken by a photographer from an airplane, back in the 1980s. It's a color photo, an aerial view of our farm, taken in the early summer or late spring. It shows wheat that was yellow gold, almost ready to cut. The corn, planted in neat long rows, is still green. There are dark brown squares of plowed ground, ready for soybeans, and some pasture with small dark spots scattered around, which were cows, grazing. This picture shows our farm property as it is today. The bank took two thousand acres of our land during the Farm Crisis, leaving us with the thousand acres I've been describing. My agriculture teacher taught us about the Farm Crisis, when a lot of farmers lost their farms because of bad crops and bad loans.

I asked Dad about the Farm Crisis once, after we talked about it in class. He gave a short laugh. "That was a bad time."

"How did we make it, when others didn't?"

"Well, we lost two-thirds of our land to the damn bank, but we survived."

I could tell it was a sore subject, so I let it go.

In the photo, the big metal shed, our new barn, glows like a big white block in the bright sun. Next to that our ginormous old barn looks tired and brown. Out in a field a tiny tractor pulls some sort of plow, with a big cloud of dirt blowing behind it in the Kansas wind. That's my dad down there, preparing to plant beans. On the day this photo was taken he was a young man with no children and a new wife. It's hard for me to imagine what he was thinking at the time the airplane flew over. Was he happy down there in his little tractor, pulling a plow? Did he dream of having a son to follow in his footsteps, to keep the farm going? Would he have stayed on that tractor all these years if he had known back then how things were going to turn out?

The thought hit me: could Alex's death mean the end of our family farm? He was supposed to take it over. Does that mean it was now up to me to be the farmer?

Looking at the picture of Dad, I thought, that could be me, driving a tractor for the rest of my life. I might be a farm girl now, but I didn't want to wind up like my parents, with all the chores and the harvests and all the worry—and the stress. That wasn't my photograph.

Grandma came in from the kitchen, smiling, looking forward to our visit. But my stomachache was suddenly worse. I stood up quickly and said, "I need to go home now."

She hugged me close and kissed me on the cheek, not questioning. I took the path toward our farmhouse, suddenly afraid of where that path might lead.

CHAPTER 8

Our house was awfully quiet in the days and weeks after the funeral. People stopped coming over like they had just after the accident. Empty pans and dishes from church folks stayed stacked on a counter in the kitchen. Sympathy cards came from people who lived out of town, including a few from people we didn't know who'd read about the accident in the newspaper.

Coach Mullins from Fort Hays State University wrote a letter. *Alex was an outstanding athlete and an even better young man, and we were very excited about him being part of our football program this fall. If there is anything I can do during this difficult and tragic time, please call...*

Alex was good at basketball and running track, but he'd chosen football because he liked the teamwork and the rush he got carrying the ball. He'd chosen Fort Hays State because they offered him a scholarship and the chance to play as a freshman. On the day he died he was in the best shape of his life. He'd been lifting weights and running every day, looking forward to his first season of college football.

Alex had confided in me that he and Betsy were planning to take a break in their relationship when he went off to college. He wanted Betsy to enjoy her senior year, to have a high school date for the homecoming dance, that sort of thing. She wanted him to find out if he really loved her by giving him the freedom to be an eligible man on campus.

They'd been going out officially since he was a high school freshman and she was in the eighth grade. But Betsy had always been in love with my brother, as long as I can remember us talking about those things. She was cute and perky and smart, and I approved of her in every way.

On the mantle above the fireplace in our living room is a photograph of Alex and Betsy at last year's homecoming. He was king, she was queen. There's also a photo of them at the prom. He wore a white tuxedo with a turquoise bowtie and cummerbund, his hair gelled just right; she wore her black hair up, with dangly earrings that matched her shimmering black dress. They look like Hollywood actors or models or something. I couldn't look at those photos without getting a lump in my throat, for Alex, and for Betsy, thinking about what might have been, for them, for all of us. There are more pictures of Alex, class photos, from one year to the next, lining the wall in the hallway of our house. They were painful for me to look at.

It was hard for me to be alone in the house now, with all these memories and all this emptiness. It was hard on my parents, too. They didn't say much about anything. My stomach still hurt. I couldn't sleep. We were all walking around like zombies. I didn't think we'd ever be alive again like we were before, when Alex was still around. I kept thinking that he'd be coming home any minute, that he wasn't really gone—forever. I could still feel his presence, like he was in the next room or just outside, not far away, even though that might sound strange. The feeling stayed with me, like an ache.

I didn't know how Betsy was feeling about Alex. She'd been hit with a double truckload of pain and grief, too. Her brother was dead, and so was the boy she'd hoped to marry. Don't get me wrong, I missed Caleb, it's just that we were never as close as Alex and Betsy had been. Caleb and I went to homecoming and prom together, and our pictures are up on that mantle too. But Caleb was not my Prince Charming. He was my best boy friend, not my boyfriend. I know he wasn't the one I was supposed to marry, despite what Betsy and I used to say about it.

While all of these thoughts and emotions were on my mind, outside in the fields, our golden wheat was ready to be harvested, which, to say the least, was going to be interesting.

CHAPTER 9

Wheat harvest wouldn't be the same without Alex. He and Dad were a really good team and had been working the harvests together since Alex was old enough to drive the grain truck. But now, with Alex gone, Dad was going to need someone to help him haul the grain to the elevator. The pit in my stomach grew deeper as I realized he needed me to help him. I drive a regular-sized pickup and I can work a stick-shift, so it wasn't out of the question that I could step in. But I'd never driven the big grain truck before.

Dad brought it up in his usual roundabout way at breakfast, saying, "Well, it looks like it's time to start cutting wheat. I'm thinking about later this morning if the weather holds."

"Do you need some help?" I asked hesitantly. "Think I could drive the big truck, maybe?"

Dad put down his coffee cup and ran his hand through his graying hair. Mom was at the stove cooking scrambled eggs. She turned to see how Dad was going to answer, her eyebrows raised. He smiled the first real smile I'd seen since before the accident.

"Well, if your mother can spare you from the kitchen, I think you could handle it. Your mother drove the grain truck for years, remember, honey?"

Mom nodded. "I think she could probably drive the big truck. We won't need her to help with the food..." She didn't finish the thought, but her smile faded. I knew she was thinking, *Now that we don't have a hungry teenage boy to feed.*

There was a stretch of silence as we all spent time thinking about Alex and what his absence would mean over the next few days of harvesting.

"Dad, I really want to try to do this," I said, even though I wasn't sure I really could.

"Okay, then," he said. "I've got time this morning to teach you how to drive the big truck."

It's hard to explain, but for the first time since the accident, I felt like doing something. I think we all did. We had a big job ahead of us, something we could do to take our minds off what none of us could stop thinking about.

Not that I thought driving the big grain truck was going to be easy. I'd had enough trouble learning to drive the pickup. I killed the engine a hundred times trying to figure out how to work the stick shift and the clutch.

"For crying out loud," Alex had teased, "you're giving me whiplash!"

"Shut up! Shut up! Shut up!" I shouted, losing my temper. I got out, slammed the door, and stomped into the house, through the kitchen and into my room, slamming that door behind me, too.

Alex knocked on my door. "Go away!" I yelled. He opened it anyway.

"Sorry about the whiplash thing. You're doing better than I did at first, really. Come back out. I'm sorry."

I blew my nose and wiped my tears, and followed him back outside.

"Let's try it in reverse," he'd said. "Push in the clutch and start the engine. Push the gear shift down and all the way over to the right, and then pull it back. Now let out the clutch slowly as you gently press on the gas."

The truck rolled backward without a jerk. "You're driving!" he said.

"I'm going backward, you moron."

We laughed and laughed.

I thought about that lesson as I sat there in the cab of the big grain truck. "Maggie? Did you hear me?" Dad said.

"Um, sorry, say again?"

"I said these gears are the same as the pickup, but the clutch is harder to push down. You'll really have to stomp on it."

I finally got it figured out after a few tries. No whiplash.

"You'll get a real leg workout working that clutch," Dad said. "But I think you'll do fine."

About mid-morning, I walked across the yard to the big shop. Dad was checking the oil in the huge red International Harvester combine, listening to the farm report on the radio.

The combine is the most complicated and expensive piece of equipment on our farm. It has a zillion chains and gears and belts and pulleys that need to work perfectly. A broken belt or busted part out in the field can cost a lot of time to fix. And time is money when getting a wheat crop out of the field.

Dad wiped his hands with a rag and turned off the radio. "Looks like a perfect day to cut wheat! Are you ready to go?"

"I think so." I was feeling pretty nervous, actually.

Dad lifted our two-way radios off the chargers and handed me one. "I'll run this other radio into the kitchen to give to your mother," he said, walking out of the shop toward the house. With the radios, we would all be able to talk to each other, because the combine has a two-way radio built into it. Dad came back to the shop and climbed up the ladder of the big combine, opened the tinted glass door, and sat down in the big driver's chair.

"Follow me out to the far southwest field. We'll start there."

He closed the door, gave a thumbs-up sign with a leather-gloved hand, and pushed the start button. The combine's engine roared to life. He checked his gauges to make sure everything was running right and shifted the combine into reverse gear.

As Dad turned the combine around in the yard, I ran over to the grain truck, reached up to open the big door, and climbed inside. I set my cooler with bottled water and snack food next to me on the bench seat, took the radio, and pushed the talk button.

"Testing, one, two, three, testing...Dad, Mom, can you hear me?"

Dad's voice came on the speaker. "I hear you, Maggie, loud and clear."

"Have a great day!" Mom said. "What time do you want me to bring dinner?"

"Well, it's about eleven o'clock now," Dad said. "Let's eat dinner at about two-thirty. That will give us enough time to get a good start."

Nervously, I put my left hand on the big steering wheel of the grain truck, pushed the clutch down hard with my left foot, fed some gas into the engine with my right, pumped the gas pedal a few times, and turned the key. The big engine roared to life, making my whole body shake. I shifted into first gear and let out the clutch as I pressed on the gas pedal, just like I'd practiced. The truck lurched forward—and died.

"Maggie?" Dad said. I picked up the radio and pushed the talk button. "What?!" I shouted, embarrassed.

"Did you release the emergency brake?"

"Oops! Right!" I slammed the radio on the seat and released the brake lever. This time as I let out the clutch and pressed on the gas, the truck lurched a little and began to move forward.

"Whew!" I said. "Here we go." I shifted into second gear and pointed the big truck down the long driveway, looking over the big steering wheel and the long hood as I rolled slowly toward the road. "So far, so good, Maggie," I said, letting out a nervous huff.

Out the windows of the tall truck, an ocean of golden wheat was waving in the wind, stunningly beautiful, under a totally blue sky. I felt a familiar pain in my stomach. I'd followed Dad's combine for many harvests in this truck, but not as the driver. That was always Alex's job. It felt different, lonely, without him as I followed the slow-moving combine down the dusty road to the first of our yet-to-be harvested fields.

About a mile later, Dad turned the giant combine off the road and drove into a wheat field. As the combine rolled into the grain, a wide row of wheat was mowed down under the slow-rolling blades. A shower of straw streamed out behind the combine, carpeting the ground with gold. I waited until Dad cut a row of grain and then pulled the truck into the field. I turned off the engine and felt the truck stop shaking. A warm breeze filled the cab, promising a sweltering summer day, maybe as hot as one hundred degrees.

I opened the cooler, pulled out a water bottle, and took a sip. *Don't drink too much,* I thought. *You'll have to pee.* When it comes to going, guys have it a lot easier than girls out here in the country.

I watched Dad's combine churn down the long row, the rumble of its engine fading away. I heard the familiar song of a meadowlark and watched the brown-and-yellow bird fly past. In the distance, an airplane made a white line across the big Kansas sky. Dad turned the combine at the end of the field and started back. My truck shook as he came by. Through the window of the combine's cockpit, I saw him pick up his radio.

"Not quite full," he said before turning the combine around.

I pressed my talk button. "How's it looking?"

"Really good, just like we expected." I saw him smile.

Several passes later, the radio squawked again. "Okay Maggie, come and get it!"

I felt a jolt of apprehension as I turned the key. The truck rumbled and bounced over the field of fresh-cut stubble. I drove about a quarter mile, wrestling the big steering wheel, to the middle of the field where Dad was standing out on the platform of the parked combine. He motioned me to come alongside. I pulled close, making sure to leave enough room for the big side mirror that stuck out from the big truck's door.

"Whoa! That's good!" Dad shouted. I pushed down on the clutch and the brake. "Turn it off but leave it in gear! Perfect!"

Dad swung the long arm of the auger over the bed of my truck and pulled a lever. The falling grain sounded like rain pounding on a metal roof. I sighed with relief. I'd done my job, so far.

It took four more combine loads before my truck was full. I handled the coming alongside better each time, without incident, and spent the time between listening to country music on the radio. Finally, the big truck was full and it was time to go to the elevator. Oh, boy.

"Take it easy driving to town," Dad said, brow furrowed. "Don't go over forty miles an hour. Don't pass anyone on the road. And for goodness' sake, Maggie, take the corners slow."

"Sure, Dad, don't worry. I've got this," I said, forcing a big fake smile. My hands were sweating as I cranked the huge steering wheel. The truck made a slow circle on the stubble, lumbering toward the road. Could I do this? I didn't know, but I was going to find out.

Over the radio, Dad announced, "Maggie's on her way with the first load."

Mom's voice came back, "Drive carefully, Maggie. We'll have dinner waiting for you when you get back."

I slowed to stop at the end of our dirt road. There was no traffic on the two-lane blacktop, thank goodness, so I pulled out and turned toward town. It took a long while to work through all four gears and get it up to forty, as loaded and heavy as it was. In the distance I could see the tall white grain elevator, eight miles ahead. The elevators are always the tallest buildings on the prairie, and, on harvest days, the busiest places in Kansas.

My mind drifted as I rolled along. My thoughts went back to other harvests when Alex was driving and I rode in the passenger seat, just tagging along. We talked about all sorts of things to pass the time. He was always good at giving me advice. I had been expecting him to help me figure out what I was going to do about picking a college, maybe a career.

I was wondering what advice he would give me now when the thought occurred to me that I might be driving a farm truck for the rest of my life. At the same instant, I heard a big thunk and the steering wheel lurched. I'd let the truck drift too far to the right. The front wheel on the passenger side had fallen off the six-inch ledge of blacktop. I heard the rumble of the right side wheels on the gravel. I turned the steering wheel back to the left but that didn't work. Next thing I knew, I was rolling toward the ditch!

I took my foot off the gas pedal and rose up from my seat, yanking the steering wheel again with all my might. The truck bounced back over the raised edge of the blacktop and veered all the way to the left, into the other lane! I yanked the steering wheel back to the right and felt the full load of grain rocking. Checking my rearview mirror, I put my foot on the brake and stopped. There was still no traffic coming in either direction.

My whole body shook as I leaned my head on the steering wheel. The whole thing had taken less than twenty seconds, but it was the longest twenty seconds of my life. Let's just say that I drove more carefully from then on, keeping my mind and the truck on the road, at thirty-five miles per hour. Lots of cars passed me before I finally reached the sign that read, "Welcome to Grain Valley," but I didn't mind.

The speed limit dropped to twenty as I got closer to the heart of town. Townsfolk sitting on store steps waved as I rolled down the main street, which is called Walnut Street in Grain Valley. I stopped at the only four-way. A poster taped to a barrel in the middle of the intersection invited all comers to a benefit supper. I rolled past the auction house, where farm tools were set out on long tables.

I bounced over several bumpy sets of railroad tracks, then turned left, into the Grain Valley Co-Op. A handwritten sign read, "Have a safe harvest! Double cropping? We have the seed you need. Open until 9:30."

I drove my truck onto the scale, a long slab of concrete outlined with a steel border, and turned the engine off. A man appeared at my window, carrying a clipboard. It was a face I'd seen before.

"Hello, Maggie!" Mr. Bright said with a smile. "Your dad called. Said you were on your way. Looks like you made it here just fine."

"Yes, sir! No problem!" I said. I wasn't about to tell him about my close call out on the blacktop. In fact, I never told anyone about that, until writing it now.

Out the back window, I saw a second man sticking a long metal tube into our load of grain. He pulled out a sample and went in the office. I watched him through a window, pouring wheat from the tube into a machine of some kind. There were no trucks waiting behind me, so there was no rush to get going. It gave Mr. Bright and me a chance to talk awhile. He held the clipboard up to me. His hands were wrapped in white gauze and white tape.

"You'll need to sign this ticket," he said. I took a pen from his bandaged hand and wrote my name.

"Be right back," he said. I watched him go inside and saw him say something to the other man. They both looked in my direction. I waved nervously, wondering if they could read my mind. The last time I'd seen Mr. Bright was at the funeral. He'd also come to the graveside service. "I'm so sorry Maggie," he'd said, like he had to apologize for something. It struck me as odd at the time. When I told Dad about it he frowned and shook his head.

"He has nothing to apologize for. He was the first responder on the scene. He burned his hands badly trying to get that truck door open. He punched out the window just as it exploded. It could've killed him. There wasn't anything else he could've done. The boys were already gone, but he still tried to get them out. He's lucky to be alive."

I thought about that as Mr. Bright handed me a yellow ticket. "Put this in your glove box and give it to your dad at the end of the day, for his records," he said. He pointed across the big gravel driveway at the grain elevator. "Drive over there. The boys'll help you unload."

Two boys I knew were waiting at the entrance of the giant grain bins. They were dressed alike in their Grain Valley High School football t-shirts with the sleeves cut off, and blue jeans and steel-toed work boots. They also wore hard-hats and sunglasses, and filter masks hung under their chins. They waved me into the shadowy opening, hollering "Whoa!" when the back of my truck was positioned just right.

One of the boys stepped up onto the side of the truck and looked inside. "Hey, Maggie." It was Clayton Dalke. He had just graduated, with Alex and Caleb.

"Hey, Clay," I said.

"You know how to tip this thing?"

"No, not really."

"No problem, scoot over." Clay opened the door and climbed in. His clothes and arms were covered with grain dust. He flipped a switch on the dashboard, and the truck bed tipped backward.

"Better roll up your window," he said, cranking up the window on his side.

I rolled up my window too, just in time. A big cloud of wheat dust billowed up like a blizzard, all around the truck, but didn't get inside. The boy in the back pounded on the truck, signaling an empty load. Clay flipped the switch, and the truck bed went back down again.

"That's all there is to it," he said. "You can do it yourself next time." He got out of the truck and closed the door. I slid back over to the driver's seat and mouthed the words "thank you" to him through the rolled-up window. He gave me a thumbs-up sign. I rolled away, feeling like I'd accomplished something pretty important.

"Good job, Maggie!" Dad said over the radio. "Mr. Bright said you handled everything just right. Your mom and Grandma have dinner ready when you get back."

As I rolled down the blacktop toward the farm, I realized that this was the same highway on which Alex and Caleb had lost their lives. My stomach churned all the way home.

CHAPTER 10

I drove down to the field where we'd been cutting. The combine was parked in the middle, and Mom's van was parked right beside it. I pulled up and shut off the engine.

"There she is!" Grandma shouted, smiling and clapping her hands. "Way to go, girl!"

I smiled nervously, not letting on. "What's for dinner?" I asked, changing the subject.

"We've got fried chicken and mashed potatoes with gravy," Grandma said, "tossed salad with fresh-cut cucumbers and tomatoes, and corn on the cob from the garden. And a loaf of fresh-baked bread, and lemonade or iced tea."

"Sounds delicious," I said, wondering if I could eat any of it.

Mom handed me an empty plate and a roll of silverware wrapped in a cloth napkin. "Dig in, eat up. There's plenty."

Harvest meals have always been a real feast in the Steele family, and this one was no exception. They'd carried the food in the same wicker picnic baskets we'd been using for years, with the same covered dishes wrapped in dish towels from the kitchen to keep them warm or cold, depending. The whole thing was set up in the back of the van. I grabbed a drumstick and a thigh and spooned a big glob of potatoes on my plate. Mom took the lid off the gravy and handed me a ladle. I made a crater and poured in the gravy. Grandma put a slab of butter on my plate and shook salt and pepper on the corn for me, like I was still a little kid.

"Oh, don't forget the salad!" she said, filling up a big bowl with fresh greens, adding some Thousand Island dressing, my favorite. "You go sit and I'll bring you something to drink. Oh, I forgot your bread! I made it fresh this morning!" She sliced off the end and put it aside, then sliced another thicker piece, buttered it, and laid it on top of my overfilled plate. "That should tide you over at least until supper."

Mom was fussing over Dad's plate the same way. We all sat down together on lawn chairs next to the combine, out of the wind. I balanced my salad bowl on the armrest and bit into the bread. The butter had started to melt. I closed my eyes, savoring it, thankful for my life.

Suddenly I was as hungry as I'd ever been before. "This is awesome!" I said, because it was.

Mom and Grandma smiled. They'd put a lot of time and effort into this meal—I knew because for as long as I could remember, I'd helped.

"Iced tea or lemonade?" Grandma asked.

"Lemonade, please," I said.

She handed me a metal tumbler filled with cold lemonade drawn from the old-time metal cooler we'd used for years. I gulped down half a glass before I took a breath.

Grandma laughed. "Lordy, child! You must be parched!"

"And famished!" I said.

I chomped the buttery corn and chewed the fried chicken clean off the bone, wiping my hands on my napkin. Looking out from where we sat, I could see about a third of the wheat field had been cut.

"We still have a lot of work to do before dark, but we've made a good start of it," Dad said.

Mom and Grandma took our empty plates and put the leftovers back in the basket. There was easily enough food left over for a hungry teenager, but if anybody else was thinking about Alex, they didn't say so.

Even as full as I was, I still felt empty. But I kept the feeling to myself.

After Mom and Grandma went back to the house, Dad said he thought I'd take two more loads to the elevator before we were finished with this field. The afternoon sun was high in the sky, and despite the constant wind it was as hot and dry as a furnace. I hadn't used the bathroom all day, but after all that lemonade, I told Dad, before we started up again, I really, really had to go. He looked surprised, then realized that I couldn't relieve myself out here in the wide open spaces.

"Okay, head to the house," he said. "I'll go ahead and get started."

I drove back to the house. Mom and Grandma were standing at the sink doing dishes. "Gotta pee!" I said, dashing to the bathroom. I washed my hands and splashed cold water on my face. I took a long look at myself in the mirror over the sink. Annoying new freckles were sprinkled across my nose and cheeks.

"Well, you almost got yourself killed today, Maggie," I said. "Ain't farming great? I mean, what would Dad and Mom ever do without you?"

Grandma was waiting for me outside the bathroom door. If she had overheard me talking to myself, she didn't let on.

"Maggie, if you don't mind, I'd like to ride in the truck with you later. Would that be all right?"

"How about you have Mom leave you with me after you bring supper?" I suggested. It was pushing a hundred degrees outside, and Grandma was no spring chicken.

"That'd be just wonderful. I have something to talk about."

"Then it's a date!" I said. I went back to the truck wondering what she had in mind.

The next load of grain went as smoothly as the first, except there were three trucks lined up in front of me when I got to the grain bins around four o'clock. Mr. Bright handed me the ticket and said, "No time to talk this time."

I could see four more trucks in my rearview mirror, waiting behind me. I dumped my own load this time. The boys gave me the thumbs-up sign. Their noses and mouths were covered by the masks they had been wearing around their necks earlier.

Several more fully loaded trucks passed me from the other direction as I headed out of town and back to the farm. I smiled and waved as they went by.

"How'd it go, Maggie?" Dad asked on the radio.

"No problems, Dad. Hadta wait in line, though."

"That's what I figured, just checking. See you in a while."

"I'm halfway home," I said. I pulled the visor down on the windshield to block the late afternoon sun.

"Maggie?" Dad said.

"Yes?"

There was a pause. "I'm real proud of you."

I smiled. "Thanks, Dad. See you in a few."

CHAPTER 11

Mom and Grandma brought supper around a quarter to seven. We stood around the back of the van, eating leftover fried chicken and tossed salad with fresh bread, too busy to sit because we were in a hurry to get the last load into the elevator before 9:30.

Grandma wore a light blue linen summer dress, with a matching scarf over her head to keep her silver hair from blowing in the wind. She looked like a living photograph from the 1950s, except for the modern walking shoes she wore everyplace she went.

Sitting in the truck in the open field, we could see for miles across the Kansas flatland. On our left, the golden sun was about to set. On our right, the darkening sky was turning purple blue as night was creeping in. We could see our farmstead glimmering in the distance in front of us. "This brings back so many good memories," Grandma said, taking it all in. "Your grandfather and his father harvested this same field, just after we got married."

"How did you get here, Grandma?" I asked.

"You mean did the stork bring me?" she teased. "Was I hatched like a bird? What do you mean?"

I laughed. "No, I mean, how did you wind up trapped here on this farm?"

She raised an eyebrow and sighed. "Oh, I met your grandfather in Kansas City a long time ago. I was working at the concession stand at the Kansas City Royale Livestock show. He wanted a Pepsi-Cola, but all we had was Coke. He wore a starched white shirt and a black string tie and a big cowboy hat. Had the bluest eyes I'd ever seen on a man. He couldn't stop staring at me. And he had the nicest smile. When he smiled at me, that did it. I would've followed him anywhere. Anywhere turned out to be right here.

"I was eighteen. Had no family. I'd just left the orphanage and was living on my own in a boarding house for a dollar a week."

"Was it hard? Growing up in a children's home?"

"It was an orphanage, I was an orphan, what can I say? But it was run by good people. We got clean clothes and plenty to eat. The Salvation Army brought us Christmas. We each got one present. And the cook, Millie, was kind and sweet. Had such an aura about her, I thought it was a halo."

"A halo? Really?"

Grandma nodded, her mind far away. "Millie worked in the kitchen. I was one of her helpers. After supper we'd talk for hours. Well, she'd talk and I'd listen as she'd read from the lessons she was learning. She was studying metaphysics. I couldn't follow most of it, but she was a very wise woman."

I'd always wondered why Grandma seemed so wise and at peace about everything. She was still talking.

"When Robert came back up to Kansas City to court me, I took him to meet Millie. Of course she took a shine to him, and he liked her. When we got married in Kansas City, she came with us to the Justice of the Peace. She was our witness."

"What was that like?"

"We got married on a Friday. Had our honeymoon at the Raphael Hotel. That was a swanky place! On Monday we drove back here, to this farm. I've been *stuck* here ever since." She smiled at me.

"Don't you wonder what your life would've been like if you hadn't spent all your time in Nowhere, Kansas?"

"Well, no. I always felt this was the place I was meant to be. You bloom where you're planted. And farming was something I could believe in."

"How's that?"

"It's the law of the universe. Seeing so much wheat come out of these fields, to me it's more than farming. It's metaphysical. That's what it is."

"What's metaphysics?" I asked.

"Maggie, the word metaphysical means more than the physical, more than the appearance of things. Although this is a very trying time for you, there is more greatness and wonder in you to be revealed. It will take time, but in the right time, more of that wonder will come out in amazing ways that you don't even expect right now."

"Okay, come and get it!" Dad's voice came over the radio, temporarily ending the conversation.

I started the truck, and we rode over to the far corner of the field. Dad emptied the last load of grain into the truck.

"See you back at the house!" he said. I nodded and shifted into gear. In the rearview mirror I watched Dad get back into the combine. He switched on the headlights, and the giant machine looked like an alien spaceship as it slowly wheeled around.

I pulled on the headlights, which shone on the stubble as we lumbered along. Grandma's happy face was illuminated by the dashboard lights. We rode along in silence until we reached the blacktop and turned toward town. Cool evening air was blowing in my window. In the distance, the lights of other combines twinkled like stars.

"I feel like Alex has been with me all day," I said.

Grandma patted my knee with her hand and left it there.

"It's all going to work out fine," she said. "You'll see."

I nodded. "Do you miss Grandpa?" I asked, sniffing.

"Oh yes, I miss him. We fit together like two spoons in a drawer. I miss seeing him around the house, but he's not gone." She pointed to her head, and to her heart. "He's always right here, and here."

I cried all the way to the elevator. I was wiping my eyes with my shirt when Mr. Bright came up to my window.

"You did real good today, Maggie," he said, handing me the yellow ticket.

Grandma leaned over from her seat. "Yes, she did a great job, didn't she?"

Mr. Bright saw me wiping my eyes. He reached into his jeans and pulled out a clean handkerchief. "Keep it," he said. "Get some rest. See you tomorrow."

I'd been having the deepest conversation I'd ever had, with the smartest person I knew, and I didn't want to miss anything. Grandma sat there for a long time as the big tires sang on the highway.

Later, as we pulled off the gravel road into the driveway, Grandma said, "If I had a message for you, it would be wrapped up in one word."

"What's that?"

"Listen."

"Listen for what?"

"For what comes next."

CHAPTER 12

The second and third days of the wheat harvest went as smoothly as the first. Dad was really happy about it. The equipment held up without breaking down even once, and after nine trips to the elevator, we had a glove box filled with yellow tickets to prove it had been one of the best crops ever.

But the morning after the harvest was over I woke up cranky. My left knee was awfully sore from pushing the heavy clutch pedal. I limped into the kitchen and sat down, feeling sorry for myself. Mom poured me a glass of orange juice. As I was drinking it, Dad said, "How about you and me go out and put some straw in the barn?"

I slammed the empty glass on the table. Dad jumped, startled.

"Maggie!" Mom said.

"That's Alex's job!" I shouted. "He should be here to do it!" I pushed away from the table, the chair crashing to the floor. I limped out of the house, slamming the screen door, and went out in the yard.

"Margaret Ann Steele!" Mom called. "Come back here this instant!"

I kept limping. The kitchen door slammed. I glanced back. Mom was following me.

"Maggie! Come back!"

I started to run. It hurt my knee, but I just kept running. Away from my Dad, away from my Mom, away from the farm, away from the pressure of trying to replace my brother, away from everything.

I ran out to the road and turned left, past the harvested wheat field, which was now an unharvested straw field. A field that would then need plowing, then fertilizing, then planting, and spraying—in other words, always in need of something. I ran about a mile past that field until I couldn't catch my breath and my legs wouldn't work anymore. I stopped in an intersection of dirt roads, where I saw my shadow. A person with her arms folded over her head like a prisoner, jailed in the middle of Nowhere, Kansas. I stood there for a long time, heaving, trying to decide what to do, which way to go. My clothes were all sweaty and gross, and I was thirsty, and hot, and my knee was killing me. So I limped, pathetically, all the way home.

When I got to our driveway, Grandma was waiting for me on her front porch. "Would you like something to drink?" she called sweetly. "Iced tea? Lemonade?"

I nodded and followed her inside. Her house was shady and cool. I collapsed on the couch. Grandma handed me a glass of lemonade in a cold metal tumbler. I took a drink, and of course it was wonderful. Grandma sat in the chair across from me, simply occupying space with me. It felt safe to tell her what was on my mind.

"Grandma, why is this happening to me? And what did we ever do to deserve any of this?"

Grandma moved over and sat next to me on the sofa. She smelled like lilacs. I continued, sobbing, "I feel like I'm going to explode inside and when I do, I won't be able to stop what comes out. I keep thinking something bad is going to happen, and then I realize it already did."

Grandma hugged me and let me cry.

"Why did they have to die? I mean, why would God do this to me, to Alex and Caleb, to all of us? How could God have done such a thing? It all sucks. That's what I think."

There was a long moment of silence. Grandma was thinking. Finally she said, "Well, I don't know why it happened. Sometimes things don't make sense. But I don't believe that God does anything bad. I believe that your brother and your boyfriend will always be part of your life. I'm sad and sorry they're gone, but they'll always be a part of you; they'll always be supporting you."

I sipped my lemonade, sniffing. Grandma handed me a tissue. "What I want you to know, Maggie, is that I love you and that I believe in you. And if you're ever looking for someone to listen, no matter how angry you may be or what you are going through, I want you to know I'm here for you, no matter what."

I leaned my head against her shoulder, allowing myself to finally just let go. She held me for a long while, then said, "I believe your life will be good and joyful again, even though I know you don't feel that way right now. Together maybe we can find a way through all of this."

"But I'm so confused. I don't know what to do. I can't take Alex's place on this farm."

Grandma nodded. "What's yours to do might not be the same as your brother, and it might not be here on this farm, but what I do know is that there is wisdom inside of you. You will know what is yours to do."

"How? How will I know?"

"I'm knowing the highest and best for you. Keep listening, and you'll know also."

I felt something shift inside me. My perspective on things was changing. "I love you Grandma."

"I love you too." She smiled. "Would you like some more lemonade?"

"Thanks, that'd be nice."

I took the path past the garden to the house. I went into the bathroom and looked in the mirror. My mascara had run, and I had dirt on my face. I looked like a sad, sweaty raccoon. I washed my face in cold water and reached for a towel, eyes closed. Mom put it in my hand. I took a long time drying my face, hiding myself from her.

She said, "You okay?"

"I think so. Where's Dad?"

"Working on the baler."

"Is he mad?" I looked at Mom. She'd been crying, too. She shook her head.

"He didn't mean to upset you. It was a misunderstanding. He's proud of you for helping with the harvest. He just thought you might want to help with the baling."

"But I don't think I'm strong enough."

"That's okay. He can hire some of the high school boys."

"Will he be upset?"

"He wanted to give you a chance, that's all."

Mom and I hugged for a long time. "I need to get out of these clothes," I said at last.

"Yes, you do," Mom said, smiling.

"I could give baling a try."

"You could if you want to, but you don't have to."

I took a long shower, braided my hair, and dressed in shorts and a t-shirt. I found Dad in the shop, working under the baler. "I do want to try to help you, with the straw," I said. "But I can't do as much as Alex did."

Dad leaned his head out, frowning. "I never expected you to take over all of the bailing work. You misunderstood me, but I don't blame you. It was my fault for not spelling it out."

"Spelling what out?"

Dad went back to tinkering with something under the machine. "I talked to the football coach a while ago. Asked him if he didn't have some boys who needed toughening up. He's sending some players over this afternoon.

"You can drive the farm truck and pull the hay rack. We'll let the boys do the lifting. We need to get most of it done in the next few days, before the rain comes. Hopefully they'll bring their own gloves, and some of them might have their own hooks. We have a pair that someone can use."

I carried the hay hooks and Alex's old work gloves over to the truck. The hooks were heavier than they looked. The work gloves were stiff and dry and reminded me of all the times Alex wore them. By the time I got to the truck, I was crying again. I used one of those gloves to dry my eyes.

This was turning out to be just like that book I'd read as a kid: a terrible, horrible, no good, very bad day.

CHAPTER 13

I went back into the house, past Alex's room. His door was open. Everything was neat and tidy, which made me smile, because it never looked that way when he was alive. Other than that, it was just like he left it. The curtains were pulled back from the double windows and sunlight flooded the room. Mom opens his door every morning, and opens the curtains. She also turns on the lamp by his bed after supper, and turns it off again before bed. Every night I hear her say, "Good night, Alex. We love you. Sleep tight," before she closes his door. It may sound creepy but it isn't. It's just like it was when Alex was alive, only now he isn't. That's the only difference.

There's a photo on the wall showing Alex in his football uniform, running right over a defender in a district playoff game, headed for a touchdown. The picture had been printed in the newspaper. I remembered that game. Alex played so hard that Friday night, he couldn't get out of bed the next morning. It was like that every week. People don't realize how much pain football players go through to be a Friday night hero, but we knew. Our hero was black and blue after every game.

When I'd asked him if it was worth it, he laughed. "If it was easy, everybody'd do it," he said. "Pain is the price of admission. It's a price I'm willing to pay."

He used cold packs to ease the swelling of a bruised elbow or twisted ankle or whatever had been banged up in the game. I limped to the kitchen and found one of those ice packs in the back of the freezer. I limped back to Alex's room and sat down on his bed. I put the ice pack on my swollen knee, wrapped an elastic strap around it, and lay back on his pillow.

Ohmygosh! I was shocked by how cold it was. I wasn't sure I could stand ten seconds of it being on there, let alone ten minutes. I looked at the clock. One minute had passed. My knee hurt worse than before! It throbbed and tingled and then... it actually started to feel *warm*. I was proud of myself for not wimping out.

Alex would have laughed hysterically if he had seen the look on my face. After ten minutes I took the ice pack off and put on jeans and my work boots. My knee was still sore, but at least I could walk without limping. It tingled for the next few minutes as I walked around the kitchen, fixing myself something to eat.

I was sitting at the table when I heard a truck rumble up to the back door and stop, followed by doors slamming. I heard another truck pull up right away, followed by another.

The football boys are here, I thought. Hopefully more than two or three of them would show up. Hopefully they would know what they were doing or we'd never get finished.

I went out the screen door to see who was in my driveway. It was Coach Wilson, head football coach of the Grain Valley Threshers.

"Heard you needed help with the haying," he said, "so I brought some reinforcements."

The coach's little son, Zack, stepped forward, pulling on his kid-sized work gloves. He wore a GV coaching cap on his head, and a toothless smile on his freckled face.

"We're going to put up all of your straw!" he lisped.

I laughed. "You are? You and what army?"

The boy pointed out to the road. More pickups were rolling up our driveway. One of them pulled a hay wagon. Another pulled a baler just like ours. The trucks stopped, and assistant football coaches got out. Meanwhile, Dad came out of the shop, and Mom came from the kitchen to welcome the men who'd coached so many of Alex's teams.

Out on the road, more trucks continued to arrive. They filled in the backyard and lined the driveway. Fathers carrying baling hooks and work gloves got out of them. There were trucks as far as I could see. Then I saw a cloud of dust out there on the same road I'd run away on that morning. Out of the dust cloud rolled the team bus, gleaming white in the midday sun. The bus looked unbelievably huge as it came up our driveway, turned a big circle, and hissed to a stop in the yard. The doors folded open. The bus driver smiled and waved. Then the varsity football players stepped down the stairs, dressed in green and gold GV practice jerseys and blue jeans.

The first player off the bus was this year's team captain, Troy Timmerman. He was by far the biggest guy in our school—a young man, really, with a nice smile and big dimples. He walked right up to Dad, shook his hand and said, "We're here to help. Whatever you need."

Suddenly, guys I'd known for years were coming up to us, just like they'd done at Alex's funeral. You hear about these things happening, and sometimes you'll see it in a Disney movie, but this was really happening. The entire football team had come to help us.

Coach Wilson said, "I figure we'll have enough boots on the ground to get you done before dark or thereabouts. We want to finish yours today so we can head to the Millers' tomorrow."

He blew his whistle. "Listen up now! Mr. Steele has some instructions. Pay attention!"

Dad took off his glasses and wiped his eyes with his bandanna. "Well, this is unexpected." Everybody laughed at his understatement. "Thank you all for coming. When I talked to Coach this morning, I had no idea. Alex was proud to be a Grain Valley Thresher. He would be proud of you for being here."

Everyone clapped and cheered.

"Baling hay, or straw, like we're doing today, isn't rocket science, but there is some danger involved," Dad continued. "You know not to horse around on a moving hay wagon, and don't you go stabbing yourself or somebody else with a hay hook. If you work smart, you'll get through with a few blisters"—he looked up at the blazing sun—"and maybe a little sunburn. Truth is there's no way we could've done this ourselves, so thank you. Thank you very much."

As I drove out to the field, Big Troy and the other linemen who had blocked for Alex last season rode in back on the hay wagon. Little Zack rode with me in the cab. We watched Dad bale the first couple of rows with the square baler. It mechanically scooped up the straw and mashed it into a rectangle held tight with nylon cords. The bales came out of the machine on a conveyor belt and dropped onto the ground every fifteen or twenty feet or so as it rolled along. In no time at all, there were thirty or forty bales ready to be picked up.

Zack ran over with a big hay hook and stabbed it into a bale. Using both hands, he pulled with all his might. The bale moved a little ways. Big Troy picked up the bale with one hand. He used the other to lift Zack and the bale of straw up together onto the wagon. They gave each other a fist bump. Everybody laughed.

"That's enough, little buddy," Troy said. "You're having too much fun. We've got a lot of work to do."

"Zack," I said, "I could use a helper to hand out the water, if that's something you'd like to do."

He smiled toothlessly. "I'm already hot and thirsty!"

We rolled along slowly as the guys picked up the hay bales and stacked them on the flatbed hay wagon. Zack talked a blue streak, about his farm animals and his 4-H projects, and his show chickens and how much he was looking forward to riding all the rides on Arm Band night at the county fair coming up in a few weeks. He also shared some juicy gossip about what the head coach was thinking about the football team's prospects this coming season.

"Daddy says he's looking for two boys to transfer in to replace your brother and Caleb, since he didn't get them for Christmas," Zack said. "He says the cupboard is bare. He's got nobody special to replace your brother as running back. Daddy says he was the best and that it's a damn shame for two fine boys to be taken like that."

I nodded. I loved Zack from that moment on. "Thank you, Zack," I said. "My brother was great, wasn't he?"

Zack nodded. "He was always nice to me when I was the water boy." And just like that, he resumed his preseason scouting report. "Dad can't bear the thought of having to rely on Scott Stark at quarterback. He says he'd bring up a sophomore to play QB if there wasn't so much politics. What's politics?"

I realized Coach Wilson must've shared his worries with his wife in the car or at the supper table, and Zack had overheard. I knew what politics he was referring to—Rev. Stark was on the school board and expected Scott to start at quarterback, no matter what. I chose my words carefully. "Politics is a word that describes a hard thing your dad is facing," I said. "But your dad's a great coach. I'm sure he'll figure it out, and the season will be great."

"Not as great as last year."

I didn't say anything, because the kid was right. It was going to be a long season.

I watched the guys in the rearview mirror as I drove slowly along, pulling the trailer behind me. They were tossing bales up to the guys on the flatbed, who stacked them neatly in place. It was pretty cool to watch them work together as a team. It didn't take long before the trailer was stacked eight bales high. Zack handed out bottles of water, saying, "Good job! Good job, good job," just like it was a game and he was the water boy. Then everybody jumped in the empty truck bed for the ride back to the barn.

Sometime back, Dad had built a big pole barn to store our straw and hay. We sold a lot of hay now, and it was easier to load it from ground level. Sometimes I thought he put up the pole barn so we could keep using the hayloft as the best place in the world to play in. But with three crews loading straw from three different fields, the pole barn was filled by seven o'clock.

As we pulled in with the final load from our field, Dad said "Sorry, Maggie, but you'll have to put your last load in the loft."

I drove the truck over to the big barn. One of the guys who'd helped stack the bales climbed up on top of the tall stacks and opened the door to the hayloft, located high on the outside wall of the barn, then jumped inside. He stuck his head out a moment later, with a smile on his face.

"Man! It's awesome up here!" he shouted. "There's a basketball court and rope swings!"

As the players unloaded the wagon, handing the bales through the opening in the barn wall, I took Zack up the ladder to the loft. He ran to the ropes and said, "Are these for climbing?" He tried to lift himself up but didn't know what he was doing.

"And for swinging," I said. "Watch this!" I climbed up a few steps on the wall ladder and swung to the other side.

"Awesome! Can I try it?"

"It takes practice to swing on a rope. But if you want to learn, you can ask your dad, and if he says it's okay, I'll teach you."

Zack's eyes brightened. "I'm coming back here! This is the greatest barn I've ever seen!"

After the straw was stacked against the far wall, some of the players clomped around, shooting baskets in their work boots. Others messed around with the ropes. Scott Stark was one of them. I hadn't seen him since he got off the bus. I knew it was the first time he'd been up in our loft because we only invited our friends up here.

Scott took a rope over to the wall, climbed one step up on the ladder, and turned around.

"Higher!" someone shouted.

Scott climbed another step, and then a couple more.

"Higher!"

He got to the top rung and turned around. It was higher than it seemed from down on the floor. I knew from experience.

The guys stomped their boots and yelled, "Jump! Jump! Jump!"

I could tell Scott was unsure of himself. But he gripped the rope tightly and jumped off the ladder. He swung across the floor, kicking wildly and out of control, smacking into the ladder on the other side. That's when he lost his grip and fell at least eight feet onto the hard-wood floor. He rolled around screaming and grabbing his ankle. I covered my mouth to keep from laughing out loud.

Everybody ran over to see if he was okay. He'd crashed face-first into the ladder. Blood was pouring out of his nose. "My hands were tired from baling," he sniffed.

His teammates carried their injured quarterback across the floor and down the ladder. It was a perfect ending to what had turned out to be an epic day. Alex would've given anything to have seen it!

CHAPTER 14

From the time I was seven, I've shown lambs at the Walnut County Fair. Showing lambs is a lot like showing dogs, only lambs are much harder to train, because...well, because they're such stupid animals. Really stupid. This is why training and showing them is so hard. But of all the things I do on the farm, this is my favorite thing of all.

The trick to showing sheep is to teach them to push against your leg, which flexes their muscles. It's like a body-building contest. That's what the judges are looking for. More important, that's how you win ribbons, trophies, and money! My bedroom is filled with trophies and ribbons and photos of me with my lambs at the county fair and other big shows, like the Kansas Junior Livestock Show, the Kansas State Fair, and the Kansas City Royale.

Back when I was little, I got in the habit of naming my lambs after the presidents of the United States. Don't ask me why, I have no idea. But I started with Ike—President Eisenhower, who was from Kansas— and Mamie, his wife. I'm proud to report that Mamie won the breeding ewe class at the county fair. In other news, Ike died, for no apparent reason. Truth is, lots of lambs die, snap!, just like that. I've had a lot of dead presidents because, well, they all wind up at the butcher's.

That's why I decided to name my last lamb Lincoln. No matter how well he did in the show ring, I knew he was going to die tragically in the end. Morbid, I know. But you just can't get attached to show lambs, because they die, randomly or otherwise, and they're dumb as turnips. But I love them.

The biggest prize is the showmanship prize. This is a chance to show how well you handle a lamb and how much you know about them. I'd always wanted to win Showmanship, but never had. First place had always gone to Dustin Farmer. Dustin looked like Brad Pitt but I still hated him because he always won. The good news was that Brad Pitt was no longer in the picture. He'd turned nineteen and was officially too old to defend his title! I felt my competitive juices flowing again, which felt strange but good. To those who don't live on a farm, that might seem weird. But I have a lot invested in my sheep.

I've worked with my lambs for two or three hours a day, every day in the spring and the summer, since I was seven. I know how to take lambs that know nothing and get them ready to show. This is pretty amazing, considering that lambs are too stupid to even recognize me from one day to the next. They care only about the blue bucket of feed I take out to them every morning.

The Walnut County Fair begins in the third week in July, always the hottest time of the year, but it's a good time for it, because the wheat harvest is over and farm parents are usually free to spend a week dedicated to their children, who are, of course, the Future of Agriculture.

On the first morning of the fair, I loaded Lincoln into a special carrying cage that fits into the back of my pickup, along with all the stuff I needed to take with me to show him. At the fairgrounds, Lincoln weighed in at exactly one hundred twenty pounds, which was not too heavy and not too light, just as I'd hoped he would be. I led him to his stall in the sheep barn. There was a lamb-shaped sign with my name on it hanging over Lincoln's stall, courtesy of the Grain Valley 4-H Club.

Usually Alex helped me get ready at these shows. He lugged the equipment and let me lead my lamb into the barn. I hadn't thought to ask Mom or Dad to help me this time. I'm sure they would've. It felt sad to be on my own.

Suddenly a deep voice behind me said, "That's an awfully extreme lamb you've got there, Maggie. That lamb has too much muscle to win at this show."

Even without turning around, I knew it was Dustin's dad, Mr. Farmer. He'd been saying the exact same thing to me for years now. Since his son always won everything anyway, he could afford to be nice to everybody else. I liked him a lot more than I liked his son.

Mr. Farmer saw that I was alone and offered to help me. He helped me carry everything from the truck and set it up next to Lincoln's pen. He didn't say much until we'd lugged it all in.

"Maggie, I just want to say how sorry I am about your brother and Caleb. It's a damn shame what happened to those boys."

There were tears in his eyes. I hadn't expected this from Mr. Farmer. I nodded and felt my stomach get tight. Everywhere I went it seemed like somebody was there to remind me that Alex was gone. Why should the fair be any different?

Mr. Farmer offered to help me shear Lincoln to get him ready to show, which was nice because Alex used to do that, too. Shearing a lamb with a pair of electric clippers is like giving a first haircut to a two year-old. No matter how many times they've been sheared, they always act like it's the first time. Most of them kick and jump and scream like they are getting killed. But not Honest Abe. With Mr. Farmer's expert help, Lincoln stood perfectly still. First I clipped him so that there was maybe a quarter of an inch of wool left on his body. Then I spent several minutes making sure it was exactly even.

"You look so handsome, Mr. Lincoln. How would you like to go to the show?" I asked. He looked at me like he'd never seen me before. Oh well.

I tied him to his pen with a sheepshank knot so that he couldn't lie down and get dirty before the show, and put a cold wet towel on his back to keep him from overheating. That's another thing I had to learn the hard way. You can't let a lamb overheat because a too-hot lamb will start panting and then faint, which is bad, because no one ever won a show with an unconscious lamb. I asked Mr. Farmer to watch Lincoln while I went to change into my clothes for the show ring. The "dressing room" was the bathroom stall in the pavilion building. I took off my shorts and dirty t-shirt and put on a new pair of tight jeans, a pearl-button sleeveless shirt with a collar, and a rhinestone belt with the buckle I won at a Missouri jackpot show. I pulled on my best pair of Ariat cowgirl boots, tied a purple ribbon into my braid, and looked at myself in the same mirror I'd checked myself in since I was seven years old. I looked great.

I walked back to the barn, past the carnival rides and the bawling calves, feeling good about my chances. A few minutes later, the loud-speaker in the sheep barn crackled: "Senior Showmanship, you're up!"

"This is it, Abe," I said. "Here we go!"

I pulled off Lincoln's halter and handed it to Mr. Farmer. I held Lincoln with my left hand under his jaw and my right hand placed firmly right behind his ears. There's a little notch there, where the neck and skull connect. It's the best way to keep control of an animal that weighs as much as I do.

Together we made our way into the ring. There were at least ten other competitors ahead of us, most of them familiar faces. The showmanship judge was an Ag teacher at a community college from another part of the state. I looked him right in the eye as we entered the ring. It's not like I was trying to stare him down or anything. I stared at him because I wanted him to know that I was in such total control of my lamb that I didn't have to pay attention to it.

The judge watched us walk our lambs around the ring one time then asked us to set them up on the far side of the arena. I made sure there was plenty of space between the lambs in front and behind us, and prepared Lincoln for inspection. I set him up and held him still. The lambs on either side of us began to fidget and jump.

The judge went down the row, asking questions, which was another chance for our lambs to get out of control. The judge stopped in front of Lincoln and me. "How much protein in this lamb's food?" he asked.

"Seven percent, sir," I said, remembering to always answer a judge's question with "sir."

"How much does he weigh?"

"One-twenty, sir."

"And what breed is your lamb?"

"He's a cross, sir, Suffolk and Hampshire."

The judge touched Lincoln's shoulders and felt his muscles, to see how well I had trained and fed him. He looked me in the eye, but he gave no clue as to how I was doing. Through it all, Lincoln stood rock steady.

The judge stepped into the middle of the ring and pointed at the showmen he wanted to join him. The trophies were on the table next to the PA stand. I had three second-place showmanship trophies in my bedroom, but no first-place ones.

The judge pointed to Susie Bakerfield and asked her to join him in the center. Her family and friends cheered from the bleachers. Then he pointed to Sam Wylie and a girl I didn't know two places down from me. After that, he called all of the showmen over, one by one, but left me and Lincoln standing all alone.

I felt bile rising in my throat. My eyes burned. I had lost!

•

The judge took the microphone but his words were fuzzy. I didn't hear anything he said until the last sentence. I'll never forget what he said.

"And now, I'm going to place the trophy in front of the best show-man in this ring."

And then he walked over and put the first place trophy in the dirt in front of me and Lincoln.

I hadn't lost. I'd won!

Mom and Dad and Grandma had arrived in time to see the whole thing. "Your brother would be so proud of you," Mom said, putting her arm around me.

"Yes," I said, "I think he is."

I don't know why I said it like that, but I felt like he was right there with us. That he was happy too.

CHAPTER 15

With the money I got for surrendering Lincoln to his inevitable doom, Mom and I went shopping for new school clothes in Wichita. For as long as I can remember it's been something we've done together, just the two of us.

"Can you believe my senior year of high school starts on Monday?" I asked as we began the two-hour drive west to Wichita.

It was the last Friday of summer, and we'd gotten into her van at the crack of dawn. Mom didn't say anything. She just nodded.

"I can't believe it's almost over. It doesn't seem that long ago that I was starting kindergarten."

Mom nodded again. I turned on the radio, pushed the scan button and watched the numbers on the dial go all the way around to the same country station Dad listens to in the shop. I turned it off.

Out the window we passed an occasional farm, but there was lots of wide open space. You could see everything or nothing, depending on how you looked at it.

"I want to go to Sheplers first," I said. Billed as "the World's Largest Western Store," Sheplers has all the latest fashions for country girls like me.

I looked forward to seeing what I could buy with $425, which was what I'd decided to spend on new clothes. Lincoln sold for $675 at the fair auction, which was waaay too much money. But the businessmen kept upping their bids.

"I have Mr. Bright to thank for making this shopping spree so special," I said. When the auctioneer had said, "Sold! To Grain Valley Co-op!" Mr. Bright had had the winning bid.

"You're quiet this morning," I said.

Mom nodded but kept her eyes on the road. I looked at her. There were crow's feet around her eyes and wrinkles around her mouth that I hadn't noticed before, and her hair had a lot more gray in it.

I looked outside at the Flint Hills for a while. When I looked back Mom was crying. Then it hit me; this was our last school shopping trip together. I had been thinking only about how my senior year was affecting me. I hadn't thought about what it meant for my mother. I reached over and took her hand. We held hands for a long time.

CHAPTER 16

Despite all my awesome new clothes, my first week as a senior wasn't what I'd expected. Not by a long shot. I don't know exactly what I was expecting exactly, but it felt like everybody else at Grain Valley had moved on with their lives, except me.

It was an awkward, lonely feeling. I mean, most people don't talk about the losses they've had, you know? Even though lots of people have lost plenty and have lots to talk about. Fact is, by the time summer was over and school started again, few people really seemed to care how I was really feeling. Oh, they were nice. They said, "Oh, Maggie! How're you doing?"

"Okay, fine" became my standard answer because most of the time, truth be told, I knew they were just being polite. They didn't really want to know. And that was okay, really. I mean, they didn't want to know about how our house had been silent all summer, or about my mother spending hours in Alex's room alone, just sitting there. They really didn't want to know about Dad's loss of appetite or how he looked like a skeleton in his baggy clothes. And they really didn't want to know how I was doing. How angry I got sometimes.

For example, it would have shocked Mrs. Lane, our nice school librarian, to hear me say, "How am I doing? Well, I have recurring nightmares that Alex and Caleb didn't die right away. Instead, I see them getting burned alive. I see Alex pounding on the window of the truck. I hear him screaming my name."

Nope. She didn't really want to know how I was doing. To know that even in the hallway on the first week of my senior year, I was lonely all the time. The only other person who might have known how I was feeling was Betsy Miller, but we weren't talking. I'm not sure why. I just hadn't said much to her, and she hadn't said much to me. Not since the funeral. With our brothers gone there was too much missing, too much emptiness. That's what I think.

When I saw her in the hallway, I pretended not to see her. She pretended not to see me. I'd say to myself, *There's Betsy!* and I wanted to say hi, but I just didn't. I heard she wasn't cheering football this season, even though she was supposed to be head cheerleader. That must've been a hard decision for her—or maybe it was really a no-brainer. At least she didn't have to go all rah-rah and pretend she was still excited about football, or anything else we used to think was cool.

I looked at her in class when she didn't know I was looking. She stared like she was a million miles away from here. I'd thought about calling her once. I opened my phone and hit the speed dial but hung up before the call went through. I mean, what was there to talk about, anyway?

When I think about the fun times the four of us had together it makes me ache. Like the time we spent at the creek on our property, two summers ago. It may seem corny, but it was a perfect rural setting, happy teenagers hanging out at the creek in the middle of the country. I can see Alex and Caleb doing tricks on the Tarzan rope Dad had hung from a high branch. After baling hay in the sun with their shirts off, the boys looked like Gap models. Betsy and I wore our hot new bikinis. Mom had taken us all the way to Wichita to shop for them.

Betsy and I sunned on a blanket, slick with suntan oil, wearing Hollywood shades, watching the guys wrestle and dunk each other. Suddenly the guys came splashing toward us, their eyes filled with mischief.

"Uh-oh! They're going to get us," Betsy said like a Southern belle in distress.

"I was hoping the same thing," I said, thinking how nice it would feel to have Caleb wrap his arms around me. I'd begun to like the attention he'd been showing.

"Oh, no!" drawled Betsy. "Stay away from me, you big strong hunk of a handsome man!" My brother was a sucker for that kind of talk.

Caleb grabbed me by the ankle, pulled me in, and dunked me. When I came up, Alex and Betsy were making out. Caleb swept his arm across the water's surface, splashing the too-hot couple.

"Get a room, you two," he said.

"Yeah," I added, "save it for later!"

Then we all took turns swinging into the water. Like a damsel in distress, Betsy squealed, "Help me! Help me!" as she swung just out of

Alex's reach. He grabbed the rope and they swung together like Tarzan and Jane. They were beautiful and handsome and happy.

I sat there in class, thinking about how much had changed.

Brrriinng! The class bell rang. Betsy closed her notebook and left. I wondered if she was as messed up and angry as I was about everything. Maybe I'd ask her. Later. Right now it was time to change classes. Time to walk the hallways. Time to change desks. One week into my senior year and it already felt like that movie *Groundhog Day.* I was stuck here with no way out of this nightmare, doing the same thing, again and again and again.

CHAPTER 17

After about a month of the same old same old, something totally strange happened to me. Somebody nominated me for homecoming queen. I don't know if it was a cruel joke or an act of charity, but I was not pleased. Which is a nice way of saying, "Are you bleeping kidding me?"

I hadn't been to a football game or even a pep rally all season. So the fact that someone had actually nominated me homecoming queen totally frosted my cookies. Not that I hadn't thought about it or imagined what it might be like. After all, Alex and Betsy had looked so stunning last fall. But they were everybody's ideal couple, the all-state athlete and the knockout cheerleader. Having those two as king and queen was one of the highlights of the school year. But this felt different. I felt like a poster child for some awful disease.

So I went to take myself off the ballot. I went to see Miss Jamison, the perky new cheerleading coach who looked like a Barbie doll. "My name is Maggie Steele," I said. "I don't want to be homecoming queen."

She taught social studies. She was new. We'd never met. She blinked her false eyelashes at me.

"I didn't give anyone permission to nominate me," I continued. "I don't want to be homecoming queen."

She patted my hand, like I was three. "Do you have a problem with rejection, honey? Get stage fright in front of large crowds?"

Several swear words went through my mind at that point, but instead of cussing her out, I started bawling. Miss Barbie handed me a tissue. I blew my nose. She didn't have a clue who I was, because she wasn't around last year. I tried to explain it to her.

"My brother, Alex Steele, was last year's homecoming king." I looked for some glimmer of recognition. She didn't recognize the name. "Um, Alex and Caleb Miller were killed in a car wreck last summer."

Her eyes got big, but there was still nobody home.

"So, I don't want to go through this. Because it would be too hard. Do you understand?"

She nodded her head yes, and then shook her head no. "You know, it's quite an *honor* just to be nominated for queen. You're very pretty, but there's very little chance you'll actually win. I mean, because there are so many *popular* girls in the running."

I didn't know whether to punch Miss Perky or kiss her dimpled cheek. I decided to reward her with a genuine smile. She was right. There was no way I could possibly win.

"I don't know," I said. "I suppose I could go through with it."

Miss Jamison shrugged. "You really have no choice, dear," she said, handing me a sheet of paper. "You see, the ballots have already been printed."

My heart sank. Sure enough, there was *Maggie Steele* listed among the other candidates. Go figure, right?

"Well, I guess that's it, then," I said. "Thank you. Have a nice day."

At least I that's what I think I said. I really don't remember what I said because my thoughts were a million miles away.

When I came in the back door, Mom was smiling at me from the stove.

"Congratulations, honey!" she said.

Dad was coming in from the hallway after washing up for supper. "Congratulations for what?" he asked.

"Maggie was nominated for homecoming queen!"

"Wonderful!" Dad said.

The local newspaper, with a picture of the homecoming royalty on the front page, was lying on the table. Oh, great, I thought.

Dad's eyebrows rose. "I don't see you in this photo."

"She's not pictured," Mom said.

"What?"

"She's not actually in the picture, Robert, but the article says she's one of the nominees." Mom brought a casserole over and set it on the table. "Why aren't you in the photo, Maggie?"

I poured myself a glass of milk and took a long, guilty gulp. I lifted the lid off the casserole dish in the middle of the table. "I'm hungry, let's eat! This looks great! How was your day, Dad? Did you get those beans cut yet?"

Mom wasn't buying it. "Maggie," she said. "Homecoming is less than a week away. You haven't said a word about this. You haven't said anything about needing a new dress or—"

"That's because I don't plan on being in the ceremony. Somebody nominated me by mistake. I tried to get my name off the ballot, but it was too late. I'm not doing it. End of story. Let's eat."

Dad put green beans and casserole on his plate and poured himself a glass of milk. Mom buttered him a piece of bread, wiping the knife back and forth several times after it was already clean. The reality of the situation was becoming clear. I didn't have to explain it. After a long silence, Dad said he needed to do something out in the shop. He put on his cap and his jacket and went out the back door. The cats followed after him, hoping for another meal.

Mom and I did everything we usually do after supper, but without saying a word. I could tell she was getting ready to say something about the situation by the way she rinsed the same plate over and over.

"You should reconsider this," she said, finally. "Because you might look back in five or ten years and be sorry you didn't participate."

I took the plate, dried it, and put it in the cupboard.

"You shouldn't give up your life because your brother is...no longer with us," she went on. That was the closest she'd ever gotten to saying that Alex was never coming back home again, no matter how many nights she left the light on for him. I waited for the thought to pass.

"But it'll suck, you know? For all of us."

Mom wiped her hands and looked straight at me, nodding a little. "Well, it might *suck*," she said, using a word I'd never heard her use before, "but it will probably suck more if you don't go through with it. I know your father would get a lot out of being your escort. I think it'd be good for all of us."

I'd been saving my best excuse for last. "But I don't have a dress."

"What about the dress you didn't wear to the prom?"

Rats! I'd forgotten about last year's prom dress disaster. I'd spilled salad dressing on my dress at the restaurant Caleb had taken me to. We'd rushed home to try to get the stain out before going to the prom-enade, but by then it had already set. So I wore an antique dress that Mom had in her closet instead. The stained dress had gone to the cleaners.

I walked down the hallway and slid open the coat closet door. The dress was still there, wrapped in the dry-cleaning bag, hanging next to Alex's GV letter jacket.

"Go see if it fits," Mom said. "I think you've lost quite a bit of weight over the summer. I might have to take it in a little."

I went to my bedroom and unwrapped the dress. It was a stunning little number, skimpy with silver sequins. Caleb had loved it. I pulled it over my head, and Mom zipped it up the back. I spun around and raised an eyebrow in her direction. It was a little loose, but it fit.

"You're so beautiful!" she said. A rush of memories overwhelmed me. Mom reached out to hold me, and we had another good cry.

"I think the boys would have wanted you to do this," Mom said, wiping her eyes.

"Okay," I said. "I'll do it. For the boys. For you, and for Dad."

"And for your future self," Mom added.

"Okay then."

We blew our noses in unison, honking like geese, which made us laugh.

CHAPTER 18

The whole town was colored green and gold for homecoming. Banners on Walnut Street lampposts read *Go Threshers!* and *Break Arma's Legs!*

At the school, gold and green crepe paper crossed overhead in the hallways. The cheerleaders had put signs on the players' lockers, such as *Trounce 'em Troy* and *Sock 'em Scott*. Every day of homecoming week we were supposed to dress up according to a theme for a contest between classes. You know the drill. We had Fifties Day on Monday, Pajama Day on Tuesday, Hat Day on Wednesday, and Super Hero Day on Thursday. Everyone was supposed to wear team colors on Friday, because there was a pep rally in the gym that afternoon. But I thought it was all pretty lame, so I just dressed normal.

Freshmen and sophomores sat on one side, juniors and seniors on the other. The Spirit Stick went to the class that cheered the loudest. I'm sure these are the same activities that happen in high schools everywhere. Funny, it all so seemed exiting and important to me last year, when Alex and Caleb were playing football. But now, sitting in the middle of it, I simply didn't care. In fact, I wouldn't have shown up at all, except I'd promised to go through with the queen candidate thing, and so I had to be there.

I sat in a folding chair on the basketball court next to the pep band, with my mind flashing back to the last time I'd sat in the same spot, at the funeral. My thoughts were far away as the band played the fight song. Each candidate stood when her name was called. When my turn came, I noticed that there was way too much clapping for me. I just waved an embarrassed wave and quickly sat down.

The Threshers had won just two of five games so far this season, which made the homecoming game against rival Arma Vikings a must-win for GV. Coach Wilson took the microphone and said some things about tonight's game ("against a very tough Arma opponent who we aren't taking lightly") and the hard work his team had put forth preparing to win ("a very important game for the whole community").

"We promise to play hard tonight," Coach said, ending his pep talk. "Thanks for your support!"

The band played the fight song again as the cheerleaders and dance team waved their pompoms. For the first time since I'd been in high school, the freshman class won the Spirit Stick. They went crazy. It was seriously the only thing that happened that made me smile.

Well, that's not totally true. I smiled again when the principal said, "I see that there's only about twenty minutes left in the school day, so I'm going to let you out early. But remember to cast your votes for queen and king on your way out."

There was a mad dash to the exits. Afterward, Miss Jamison came up to me and said, "Well, if it isn't Miss Steele." I could tell she was still upset that I hadn't bothered to show up for the photo. "Will we see you tonight?" she asked frostily.

I smiled and said, "I'll be there."

She smiled back, like we were BFFs, best friends forever.

As she walked away, someone tapped me on the shoulder. It was Betsy. She looked happy. "Hey!" I said. It had been a long time since I'd seen her smile.

"I just wanted to say good luck tonight. I mean, I know it won't be easy."

We both knew how true that was. "Mom talked me into it," I said. "Says I need to start living again."

There was an awkward silence. We hadn't spoken to each other in such a long time.

"I nominated you," she said finally.

"You did? How come?"

Betsy shrugged. "I guess because I wanted to see you out there. Maybe your mom is right."

I didn't know what to say, so I gave her a hug, as students moved around us carrying band instruments and music stands. It felt good to have a friend again.

"See you tonight?" I asked.

"Wouldn't miss it!" she said.

Talk about unexpected surprises. Who would've guessed that Betsy had nominated me? After all we'd been through? It had been a week of messed-up emotions. I had a nervous lump in my throat on the way home. My nervousness grew into a near panic as I changed into my homecoming dress, and rode with my parents back into town.

CHAPTER 19

Amid all the hustle-bustle of homecoming week, I guess somebody forgot to tell the Grain Valley varsity that they would have an opponent to face, ready to spoil the evening's festivities.

Arma was playing inspired football, eager to avenge the beat-downs they'd suffered over the past four seasons. We should have been ahead by two or three touchdowns, but the scoreboard read 7–7. We were getting our tails kicked, and Scott Stark was a big part of the problem. He'd bobbled the snap twice, and Coach Wilson was really upset with him. When the whistle blew, ending the first half, Scott was curled up in a heap over another fumble. Coach Wilson threw his hat down and pointed his team to the end zone. The players took a knee and pulled off their helmets. Little Zack handed out water bottles and pounded them on their shoulder pads.

The homecoming court had been seated on the front row of the bleachers. And now it was time for the ceremony. As we stood and walked down the stairs to the track, somebody whistled loudly and shouted, "Go Threshers!" and everybody laughed.

Dad was waiting on the track to escort me onto the field, a big smile on his face. "You look beautiful," he said.

I felt like a nervous wreck. I was about to ask Dad to escort me back off the field when Miss Jamison's voice came on the public address system. "Welcome to the Grain Valley Homecoming king and queen coronation ceremony!"

"Oh, brother," I said.

"You'll do fine," Dad said, squeezing my arm. My mind drifted back to last year's ceremony and all that'd happened since then.

Miss Jamison was introducing somebody. "Gretchen is a three-year starter on the volleyball team. She's a member of Fellowship of Christian Athletes and active in the Prairie View Baptist church. She plans to go on a mission trip to New Orleans after graduating and to major in physical therapy at Pittsburg State University. She is the daughter of..."

I looked into the stands and found Betsy sitting with her parents. *Thanks a lot for the nomination,* I thought.

"The Millers are here," I said. Dad waved and they waved back.

We waited arm-in-arm as the other queen candidates were introduced. Two of them were varsity cheerleaders. The others were two volleyball players and a girl who played point guard on the basketball team. Finally there was me, the sympathy candidate who didn't play sports, or cheer, or do much of anything at school.

"Our final homecoming queen candidate is Maggie Steele."

The crowd clapped for a really long time as Dad escorted me into position on the thirty-five yard line. "Maggie is a longtime member of the Grain Valley 4-H Club, and this past summer she won the Senior Lamb Showmanship Contest at the Walnut County Fair. Maggie is undecided about her plans after graduation. She is the daughter of Robert and Barbara Steele and the granddaughter of Ruth Steele. She is escorted by her father, Robert Steele.

"Please give one more round of applause for all the queen candidates."

The king candidates were introduced next. Big Troy and Scott wore their football uniforms without their helmets, and another guy wore his band uniform. But the other three candidates looked handsome in their suits and ties.

The dads had left the field as the king candidates were introduced. Big Troy came over and stood beside me. I put my hand in his elbow.

"You look great!" Troy said.

"Well, you're sweaty and gross and you stink!" I said with a smile. We shared a laugh under the glare of the stadium lights.

Zack Wilson and a little girl I didn't know were introduced as the junior homecoming attendants. They carried the crowns on shiny gold pillows. Then Miss Jamison said, "This year's homecoming king is... Scott Stark!"

There was a big cheer from the crowd, like he'd finally scored a touchdown.

"Oh, brother!" I said under my breath, clapping politely.

Troy nodded. "No kidding."

Scott walked to the fifty-yard line with a big smile on his face. I noticed that his uniform had grass stains on the butt, and I wondered if his swelled head would fit back into his helmet for the second half.

Miss Jamison's voice came back on. "And now, I would like to announce this year's homecoming queen."

"Get ready," Troy whispered to me.

"What?"

"This year's Grain Valley homecoming queen is...Maggie Steele!"

I felt my breath squeezed out of me. Troy was hugging me against his sweaty jersey, which felt gross. Then he kissed me on the cheek, which felt amazing.

"Get over there and get your crown," he said, moving me from my frozen position. The crowd was on its feet, cheering. I walked over to the center of the field where Scott was standing. He was clapping and smiling at me. The kids stepped up with the crowns. I put the king's crown on Scott's head, and I swear it barely fit.

Scott reached over and picked up my queen's tiara. I smiled, thinking, *Don't fumble it!*

As Scott put the tiara on my head, a photographer rushed in. Someone yelled, "Kiss her!" But just as he leaned in to kiss me, I raised my hand to block my cheek and the strobe flashed.

Scott escorted me to the sidelines and over to my throne, which was really just a big, overstuffed, gold-colored chair. And then the second half started. King Scott threw an interception late in the fourth quarter that killed our chances. We lost, 14–7. After the game, lots of people came up to congratulate me, including Betsy and her parents.

Betsy hung around and we talked a little. "Good job shutting Romeo down, again!" she said. We laughed like it was old times.

Miss Jamison came over after the crowd had dwindled to a few people. "Well," she said. "I'm glad I printed the ballots before you came to see me!" She was all smiles.

"Me too," I said.

"I wanted to say that I'm sorry for not knowing your history. I understand now."

"That's okay," I said. "You had no idea. This was nice. I never expected to win."

"Really?" she said. "You got nearly all the votes."

"Unbelievable. Well, thank you very much."

As I walked toward the parking lot with my parents, Miss Jamison called out, "But you should have let Scott kiss you. He's so handsome!"

Without turning around, I let out a laugh and shouted, "No way was that going to happen!"

Mom squeezed my hand.

CHAPTER 20

We rode home from the game in happy silence. We felt like a family again, because Alex's presence was with us in the van. At home, I changed into jeans and a sweatshirt, and then hung my dress back up in the hall closet next to Alex's letter jacket.

"That was fun," I said. "I wish you'd been here to see it."

Mom and Dad went to bed. I put on my flannel chore jacket and headed out to the barn, closing the screen door softly. I walked under the cool, starry sky, a cat twining around my legs, across the yard to the old barn, unlatched the door, and went in. I climbed up the ladder to the hayloft and switched on the lights.

I'd felt Alex's presence all night. Now I felt like if I said something that he'd be right here to listen to me. I walked across the wooden floor and held one of the rope swings in my hands. I took a few quick steps and jumped on. The buckle squeaked high in the rafters as I swung back and forth.

"Hey, Alex," I said. "It was quite an evening. Wish you could've been here."

"You looked beautiful tonight."

I stopped swinging, "What? What did you say?"

A familiar voice came out of the silence. "I said you looked beautiful, Miss Grain Valley Homecoming Queen. Great job, keeping Scott from kissing you. It was another epic rejection. Just like fifth grade!"

My legs felt weak. My head was spinning. I sat right down on the wooden floor. Clearly this wasn't really happening. It was my brother's voice! It sounded like he was right there with me.

"Where...where are you?" I asked, looking around.

"I'm right here, silly. Can't you see me?"

"I can hear you, but I can't see you."

"Take the rope and climb the ladder."

I walked over to the wall, climbed up a few steps, and turned around. "Now what?"

"Let's see if you remember how to swing on that thing."

I rocked back against the ladder, feeling like I was going to faint. I wiped my sweaty hands on my jeans, regripped the rope, and swung to the other side.

"Nice! I think you've gotten stronger from doing my chores all summer."

I couldn't catch my breath. Alex kept talking to me. "You did great with the harvest and the haying. And congratulations on winning Showmanship! Lincoln was outstanding!"

I felt dizzy to say the least. "You were there? All summer? You saw everything?"

"Of course. I've really never left."

I climbed down from the ladder and sat on a bale of straw. My world was spinning.

"By the way, Grandma is right."

"Right about what?"

"About you, and your future. She told you that your harvest is coming, and she's right. You were voted homecoming queen, and that's just the start. I'm glad you went through with it."

"Is this really happening, or is this just in my head?"

"It's really happening, just in your head."

"But I mean, is it real?"

"As real as real can get."

I pulled up the sleeve on my sweatshirt and pinched my arm, as hard as I could, to see if I was dreaming. "Ouch!"

I heard Alex's laughter echoing again. And that's when I started crying. I wept a puddle of tears on the hardwood floor. I lay down on the straw and wiped my eyes with my sleeve.

Looking up into the dark rafters of the barn, I said, "I have so much to talk to you about, so many questions."

"Ask away, Sis. I've got all the answers now."

I didn't know where to start, so I said, "Well, what about the accident? Did it hurt a lot?"

Silence. I was afraid I'd offended him.

"Yes, it did hurt," he said at last, "and then it didn't. And since it didn't hurt anymore, it didn't matter that it had hurt so much. Does that make sense?"

I nodded at the rafters, sniffing. More silence. "So where are you, exactly?"

"I'm right here with you. I've been with you ever since I crossed over to this place."

"Are you in heaven?"

"You could say that. I can't wait to share it with you. To show it to you."

"You're going to show me heaven?"

"As much as I can, when you're ready for it."

"Don't I have to die first?"

"You're not dead at this moment, are you?"

I pinched myself again, but not as hard. If this was a dream, I didn't want to wake up.

CHAPTER 21

The next thing I knew, I heard the screen door slam and Mom calling my name. It took a moment for me to figure out where I was. I was still trying to figure out what had happened as I climbed down the ladder. I opened the barn door to a brand new sun-shiny day. If what I thought had happened up there had really happened, my world would never be the same.

Mom met me at the back door, eyebrows raised.

"Guess I fell asleep up there," I said. "We—I mean, I was out there on the rope swing, and the next thing I knew, it was morning. Gee, those pancakes smell great!"

"What are you so happy about?" Dad asked as he pulled out his chair and sat down.

I smothered my pancakes with butter and hot syrup and took a bite. "Oh, nothing," I said, tasting the sweetness. "It just feels so good to be queen!" I pulled up the sleeve of my sweatshirt.

"What happened to you?" Mom asked, seeing the bruise on my arm.

"It got pinched last night. No big deal, really." I pulled my sleeve down quickly.

Dad and Mom were waiting for me to say something else. I just covered my grin with a glass of cold milk and drank it all down. Milk had never tasted so delicious. To keep from having to explain, I poured myself another glass. "Thirsty!" I said, letting out a long "ahhhh!"

After a second helping of pancakes and a third glass of milk, I went down the hall to Alex's bedroom. I stepped inside the open door, feeling the same presence I'd felt in the loft. I felt like saying something to him, but didn't because Mom and Dad were still in the kitchen.

I pulled Alex's scrapbook off the bookshelf, sat down on his desk chair, and began turning the pages. The book was filled with stories and photos from the sports he'd excelled in, football, basketball and track. The headlines told the story of a short life, well lived.

Steele's 2 TD's lead GV to victory

GV takes Paola in shocker, Steele runs for 200 yards, 3 TD's

GV's Steele earns all-state honors

Steele signs with Fort Hays State

The last articles of the scrapbook had been put in there by Mom.

Two Grain Valley youths killed in highway crash

Township mourns as teens laid to rest There were several empty pages left. I closed the book, sighed a heavy sigh, and put it back on the shelf. That's when another book caught my eye, an old paperback titled *Track and Field for Boys*.

A voice boomed in my head, "Now there's a book you should take a look at, starting on page seventy-four."

I nearly fell out of the chair. It was Alex again!

"Man alive!" I said. "How about a warning or something!"

"What's that, Maggie?" Mom called from the kitchen.

"Oh, nothing, Mom." I looked around the room and whispered, "Are you out of your mind?"

"In a manner of speaking, yes. But you really should take a look at that book, then meet me in the loft sometime. I look forward to seeing you there. Peace out."

"Peace out? What's that supposed to mean?" I said, still whispering. I waited for Alex to answer, but there was no reply. As I stood up to leave, Mom passed by the doorway, carrying a load of laundry.

"Is everything all right in there, Maggie?"

I hid the track book behind my back. "Sure, why?"

"I thought I heard you talking to someone in here. What's that behind your back?"

I showed her the book.

"*Track and Field for Boys*?" she asked. "I think your father got that when he was a little boy. He gave it to your brother. It's been around for a long time."

I opened the book and turned some pages. There were lots of old black-and-white photos of boys from another generation, dressed in old-time track shorts and tank tops, doing track and field events the old-fashioned way.

"Copyright 1960. Man, this book is an antique!"

"Your brother loved that book. He and Caleb put on a whole track meet one summer, when the Olympics were on. They ran around the circle drive and Dad started them off by firing his rifle as a starting gun. They had a shot put ring and a pole vault pit and everything."

I nodded as she spoke, remembering that Betsy and I had been more interested in watching the boys compete than in doing any of the events ourselves.

I turned to page seventy-four. It was the chapter on pole vaulting. "They had a pole vault set up?" I asked.

"Don't you remember? Your dad bought pole vault stuff at the school auction. The boys kept at it all summer, and then they took everything up into the loft and did it all winter long. It was hard for them because they were so little at the time. They gave it up after awhile."

A forgotten chapter of my life was coming back to me. I needed to be alone with this book.

"Um, I think I'm going to take a nap," I said, walking toward my room. "It looks like this will put me to sleep."

I closed my door and flopped down on my bed. I reopened the book to the place I'd marked with my finger and began to read. Back when this book was published, the sport of pole vaulting had been a male-only activity. But that all changed a few years ago. I'd seen women pole-vaulters on TV. They looked graceful and daring, and I remember wondering if I could do that. I fell asleep, imagining myself as a pole-vaulter.

When I woke up, my clock read 4:35. I'd slept all afternoon. I went in to take a shower and laughed at myself in the mirror. I still had my homecoming queen makeup on. My mascara was streaked. "Dracula Queen!" I said to my reflection. "How's it going?"

"Vell," I answered in my best Dracula voice, "dat's an interesting question. Da answer you vouldn't believe!"

After a long shower I braided my hair, put on my old sweatpants, sweatshirt, and my Brooks running shoes from gym class. Mom and Dad were waiting for me in the kitchen. Supper was on the table. "Boy, I must've really been tired!" I said, sitting down.

They looked at me, expecting more.

"I mean, last night was so exhausting—what?"

Something else was going on. Mom handed me the newspaper. Dad grinned into his water glass and motioned for me to take a look at the front page. There was a picture of the new homecoming king and queen, in the exact same spot as Alex and Betsy had been the year before.

The caption read, "Stiff-armed!" It showed Scott kissing me, on the palm of my outstretched hand. The look on my face was priceless. It was an epic photo, destined to be put on the mantel. We joked about it all through supper. Dad kept pretending to stiff-arm someone. It'd been a long time since we'd laughed about anything. I couldn't wait to get back up to the loft to tell Alex.

CHAPTER 22

I snuck back out to the barn right after supper. A couple of cats followed me up into the loft. I lifted the old track book up toward the rafters and started to jabber.

"Hey, Alex! I brought the book. Am I supposed to start pole-vaulting? I tried to make sense of the instructions but I didn't understand them. It seems like a lot to learn. How am I going to pole-vault up here? I don't even have a pole!"

I heard a familiar laugh. It sounded wonderful. Alex's voice came from the other end of the loft. "Check over here."

There was a wall of straw bales over there. His voice was coming from somewhere behind it.

"Where are you?" I asked.

"I'm back here. Think you're strong enough to move these bales out of the way?"

I climbed up and pulled down one bale of straw from the top of the wall, and then another. When I finally got them all moved, I could see an old pile of loose straw on the floor on the other side.

"Hey! This is where you and Caleb used to pole-vault!"

"That's right. Come and look behind the straw pile. You'll find everything you need."

I found two long boards on the ground against the wall, dusty and partially covered with straw. "Those are the standards," Alex said.

"But what about a pole?"

"Dig around a little. It's there."

I reached into the loose straw and found what looked like an old bamboo fishing pole.

"That's an antique piece of sporting equipment," Alex said.

"You mean this is a real pole?"

"Yes, it's real. Bamboo was once considered the best pole for pole vaulting. It's lightweight and resilient, which means it has some give to it. You'll see."

The pole was about twelve feet long, and thicker at the bottom than the top. It had been wrapped a long time ago with white athletic tape, sticky side out. There was ground-in dirt and hay on the sticky part, but when I touched it, it didn't feel sticky anymore.

"You should peel that old tape off of there. You'll find a fresh roll of tape in my top dresser drawer. Bring it with you next time. You won't need it for today's lesson."

"You're really going to teach me to pole-vault? Up here, in the loft?"

"If you're willing, I am."

It might be difficult to imagine a hayloft big enough to pole-vault in, but let me assure you, it is plenty big enough. It's half as big as my high school gym. I felt excited as I unwrapped the old tape, with a little help from one of the cats, who pounced on it like it was a snake. The sticky stuff had turned to powder which fell as I untwisted the tape. After getting the tape off, I used my sweatshirt to wipe off the rest of it. The pole was quite a bit thicker than any of the bamboo poles I'd ever fished with. There was a white rubber cap on the bottom of it.

"What's that?" I asked.

"Dad put that on there. It's really made to keep chair legs from scratching up the floor, but it works great as a pole tip."

"Okay, now what?"

"Now you need to find the box."

"What box?"

"The planting box. Look on the floor in front of the straw pile."

I stepped to the other side of the pile, bringing the pole with me.

"I don't see a box."

"See that ring on the floor? Pull on it."

I reached down and pulled on a metal ring that was screwed onto the floor. I hadn't noticed it before. It was attached to a rectangular piece of wood, which covered a sloping metal box hidden under the floor.

"Dad bought that at the school auction. He put it in there."

I took the pole and stuck it into the box. "Pretty cool!" I said. "But I don't have a clue how to do this."

"Well, let's open the book and get started," Alex said.

I'd been carrying the book in the pocket of my hoodie. I pulled it out, resting the pole on my shoulder to free up both hands, because I couldn't hold the pole and the book at the same time.

"I don't think is going to work," I said.

"Why don't you set the book down and let me teach you?"

I set the book on a hay bale, cracking the old spine open flat.

"Okay, great guru of pole vaulting, I'm ready to start. Teach me!"

"Our journey begins with a single step, or in your case, with the right handgrip..."

And that's how it all began.

CHAPTER 23

Let it be known that the first time I tried to pole-vault, things didn't go so well. I took a few running steps like I was about to swing on the rope. I raised the pole over my head and stuck the pole in the plant box. The pole jerked, I lost my grip, and I fell flat on my back on the hard wood floor.

In other words, my first vault was an epic fail that knocked the wind out of me.

"Are you all right?" Alex said.

All I could manage to say was "Ugh."

"Do you want me to call 9-1-1?" he asked.

I laughed out loud, because I'd said the same thing to him when he'd fallen off the rope swing years before. I made up my mind to do the same thing he'd done back then. I was hurting, but I wasn't injured. So I got back up and tried again.

"Learning to coordinate your plant just as your left foot jumps off the ground will take some time, but you'll get the hang of it. Make sure your left foot is in line with your top hand, directly underneath it when you take off. If your foot is too far behind your top hand, you'll lunge at the box and it will throw you off balance. On the other hand, if your takeoff foot is too far in front of your top hand, your shoulder will feel like it's being jerked out of the socket. You'll lose your momentum and stall out. It's called being under."

"Oh, that's what it's called," I wheezed. "Being under, stalling out—and crashing! I think you left out the crashing part!"

"Want to try it again?"

"Sure, but I don't want to crash again. What did I do wrong?"

"Just hold a little lower on the pole, then ride it into the straw."

I tried it again, just like he said. I rode the pole and landed on my feet in the straw.

"Ta da!" I shouted, feeling very proud of myself.

"Way to go, Sis! But I forgot to tell you, never land on your feet. You don't want to twist a knee or an ankle. Just land on your back or your rear, it's safer that way."

"If I'm going to risk landing on my backside, I'm going to need more straw!"

Alex laughed. "This is a good time to quit for the day anyway. You can pile up more straw next time."

After my first lesson, my hands were tired and crampy from grabbing the pole. My shoulder felt like it had been jerked half way out of the socket, and my backside was sore. But I felt like I'd done something pretty special as I walked back across the yard to the house.

Mom and Dad were at the table, paying bills. Mom had the checkbook. Dad had a calculator. Papers were stacked in piles. I figured they were too busy to talk, so I headed to my room to change clothes.

"What on earth have you been doing?" Mom said. "Your backside is covered with dirt!"

I stopped, not knowing what to say. "Um, I was just messing around on the rope swing and kind of fell on my back. I'm a little out of practice. Don't worry, I'm not hurt. Knocked the wind out of me a little, that's all."

"Are you sure?" Dad said. "Come here and let us take a look at you."

I walked back to the table and crossed my eyes. "See, nothing wrong with me!" I said in a crazy voice. "Except I'm seeing double!"

"Hit the shower, goofball, you smell a little ripe," he said.

I punched Dad on the shoulder. "Hey, I took a shower sometime last week!"

I walked to the bathroom, pulled off my dirty hoodie, and put it in the laundry basket. Whew! I couldn't tell them I'd been learning to pole-vault because they would ask why, and I couldn't say, "Well, because Alex thinks I'd be good at it." No, I couldn't go there. Not now, maybe not ever.

I tried talking to Alex in my room after supper, asking if we could practice again tomorrow. I felt his presence like always, but got no answer. "Aren't you going to say something?" Silence.

"Giving me the old silent treatment, eh?" I tried humor. "What's the matter, cat got your tongue?" I tried logic. "Certainly it's possible for you to hear me and speak to me here as well as in the barn, since you are everywhere present, right?" I tried pity. "For crying out loud, what does it take for me to get my brother to speak to me from the great beyond?" But Alex didn't answer. It was late, and I was tired. I figured if Alex didn't want to talk to me here, he must have his reasons.

"Well, good night then." I turned out the light, hoping to hear him say, "Good night, Sis," like he'd done so many times before. But all I heard was the wind, rustling the dry autumn leaves on the tree outside my window.

I thought about what Alex had told me today, in our lesson. I wondered what the future might bring. I'd been thinking of my future as something random, beyond my control. But Alex had said, "You can do whatever you want to do, be whoever you want to be, if you are willing to see it through."

That night I dreamed I was flying over a giant harvest moon. A canopy of stars twinkled over my head. It was beautiful.

CHAPTER 24

The days and weeks after homecoming went quickly, at school, on the farm, and up in the loft. The football team won its last two regular season games, but was knocked out in the first round of the playoffs. It was the first first-round loss anyone could remember, and the first losing season since who knew when.

My classes were challenging, especially AP science and calculus, which was really kicking my butt. After the first nine weeks I was struggling to make Cs in both of those courses. I got an A in AP English and a B in American history, and of course, an A in vocal music.

My least favorite class was advanced agronomy, even though I was making an A. The more I learned about the business of agriculture, the more afraid I became. Traditional family farms like ours are mostly a thing of the past. Today's corporate-owned farms are so big and harvest on such a large scale that our thousand-acre farm is tiny by comparison. It's hard to explain, but bottom line, it's hard to make money on a small-scale operation like ours. No wonder so many farmers have ulcers and heart problems—just studying about it gives me a stomachache. I wrote a term paper on the Farm Crisis of the 1980s, which was a really bad time. What I learned in class was what Mom and Dad had experienced and were still experiencing every day. Now, with Alex out of the picture, the clock was ticking on the biggest decision of my life.

Most people don't give a flip about this farm stuff. But if you think about it, everything you eat that you don't grow yourself probably came from a farm like ours. There are more and more people being born into this world every day, and fewer farmers to feed them. I think people should think about that when they sit down to eat Thanksgiving dinner this year. If I decide not to keep farming, then someone else will need to take over our farm and grow crops. But most people don't give these things a second thought. They think food comes from the grocery store. That's all they know or care to know. Truth is, no farmers, no food. Just saying.

Anyway, I helped Dad harvest soybeans. We did the cutting on the weekends throughout November, leading up to Thanksgiving. Soybeans aren't a big deal to harvest, because they can sit in the field until they are cut. I drove the grain truck to the elevator with no problems.

We ate Thanksgiving dinner with Grandma. Mom put a setting at Alex's place. We took some time going around the table, telling what we were thankful for, and everybody said something they remembered about him. It was happy and sad at the same time, but mostly happy.

I was vaulting almost every day. After school, I'd rush home to change clothes and hurry up to the loft. I couldn't wait to spend time with Alex, figuring out this pole vaulting thing.

We did every vault from two steps or four steps at first. It took a long time to learn, but Alex said we couldn't go any further until I'd figured out how to stay balanced, to ride the pole without spinning out of control. To do this, I had to line up my body so my belly button, or center of gravity, was directly behind the pole.

I must have taken a hundred little jumps like that to figure it out, but finally I was getting the hang of it, landing straight every time.

"You're a great coach," I said.

"That's just because I know everything," he said. "The mystery of the universe is no longer a secret to me, which makes coaching even something as complicated as pole vaulting seem pretty easy, relatively speaking."

I'd pole-vaulted into the straw for several practices before Alex said I was finally ready to jump over the crossbar. By that time I'd been taking practice vaults from six steps away from the box. In addition to staying well balanced, Alex was teaching me to keep every step consistent on my run-up.

The old standards were made of cast iron, which meant that they were ridiculously heavy. I struggled to put them in place on either side of the straw pile.

"I could use a little help here!" I said to Alex as I dragged a standard into place. "Why don't you get off your butt and help?"

"Gosh, I wish I could," he said.

"I bet."

The pegs on the standards started at six feet. I knew this because someone had written a big six with a marker. The pegs went up six inches at a time, all the way up to twelve feet, which looked impossibly high.

"Set the crossbar on the lowest peg," Alex said. "But before you jump, put your pole in the box to see how the standards are set."

The crossbar was about twelve feet long and surprisingly light. It was made of some kind of lightweight metal like aluminum. The crossbar was crooked in some places, but it was mostly straight. It was painted black and white and had three sides, so it looked like a triangle on the ends.

I set the crossbar on the lowest peg of one standard and then the other, and put my pole in the box like Alex said.

"Hold the pole straight up and down, I need to see something," he said. "Okay, now move the standards about a foot further back, away from the box."

When I scooted the standards, the bar fell off and hit me on the head. "Ow! That hurt! How about a little warning?"

"Watch out!" Alex said, laughing at his own joke.

"Yeah, a little late!" I rubbed my sore head and pulled the other standard into place. Then I put the crossbar back on—lesson learned.

Six feet seemed pretty high. It was about four inches over my head. My throat began to feel tight. I was about to make the first real vault of my life.

"Are you sure I'm ready for this?" I asked.

"Don't think about the crossbar," Alex said. "It's easy to say but hard to do."

I walked back to my starting mark. Alex continued to coach me. "Just keep doing what you're doing. You're already going that high in the air."

I stood at my takeoff mark and looked down the runway at the bar. My hands were sweaty, so I wiped them on the front of my sweatshirt and regripped the pole. I took a deep breath and let it out in a huff. I stood at my mark, pretending to push my top hand up into the plant position, lifting my right knee like I'd been practicing for weeks. Only this time, there was a real bar up there!

Now or never, I said to myself.

I lifted the pole and ran down the runway, getting faster as I neared the box. Three...two...one! I reached my hands up to plant and leapt off my left foot, just like before.

I rode the pole straight down the middle. When I pushed the pole away and fell on my back in the straw, the bar was still up there!

"Bravo! Way to go, Sis!"

"Woo-hoo!" I shouted, doing a little dance. "I can't believe I just did that!"

"You did it! Great! Your concentration is good. The crossbar scares a lot of people but it didn't scare you! Actually, you were way over it. You should raise it six inches and go again."

I jumped out of the straw and set the crossbar up one peg higher on each side. I was cranked. It felt like electricity was buzzing through me.

I ran to the top of the runway with my pole. But when I got there I was so excited, I could hardly catch my breath.

"Take your time. Don't get in a hurry. Hold an inch higher on the pole. Try to do everything just like you did the last time."

"Okay, got it!" I took a deep breath and blew it out.

My second real vault was even better than the first one. I clapped and shouted when I landed, throwing up handfuls of straw.

"Easy-peasy!" Alex said. "Let's raise it up to seven feet!"

It was a stretch for me to put the bar up to seven feet, but I got it up there. My heart was still pounding out of my chest. I felt so alive and happy. This was the coolest thing I'd ever done!

"Seven feet!" I shouted.

"Even as the bar goes up, keep doing it the same way you've been doing."

I ran down the runway, planted the pole, and jumped off the ground. A thousand rope swings had prepared me for this moment. My grip felt strong. I rode the pole to the vertical position, raising my knees to my chest. The bar bounced on the pegs as I fell backward and landed in the straw. I closed my eyes to keep the dust out, but when I peeked I saw the bar hadn't fallen down.

"Great job!" Alex shouted.

"Whew! That was close," I said. "What did I do wrong?"

"You didn't do anything wrong, Maggie. You just vaulted seven feet! It takes a lot of doing the right things to jump that high on your first day. We can make some adjustments next time. But I want you to enjoy this feeling. I'm proud of you. Let's call it a day."

I was disappointed that Alex wanted to stop, but I felt super great about what we'd just accomplished. I stayed there in the straw, looking up at the crossbar. I felt very successful, like I could do even better tomorrow.

"Thank you Alex."

"Don't mention it. You did great. The sky's the limit for you, Sis, you're a natural."

I was still buzzing when I went to bed. I could still feel what it felt like to go over a real crossbar. It took a long time to fall asleep. I dreamed I was flying over a harvest moon, just like before. Only this time I was pole-vaulting, over the moon and into the stars.

CHAPTER 25

Next morning at the breakfast table, Mom said, "Maggie, why are you smiling?"

"Oh, no reason," I said, but I was thinking, *Because I'm in love with pole vaulting!*

The same thing happened in class. The teachers would call on me, but I wouldn't be paying attention. I was so excited about pole vaulting, I couldn't stop thinking about it.

"Miss Steele, would you care to join us?" they said. But I was thinking, *Not really, I'd rather be vaulting!*

When I walked down the hall, people thought I was smiling at them, but I was smiling about pole vaulting!

I started comparing how high I'd vaulted with everyday objects. Like, I could vault over my pickup truck, no problem. I could vault over that doorway, no sweat. And I could vault over that tall handsome guy walking up to me in the hallway.

"Hey, Big Troy!"

"Hey, Maggie! What's going on? You seem unusually happy lately. You're not doing drugs or something are you?"

I laughed. "OMG, Troy! Drugs! Me? Really? Of course not!"

"Honestly?" he asked, eyebrows raised. "Because the way you've been acting, some people think you've been getting high."

"Oh, I have been getting high, and I plan to go a lot higher," I said, watching his eyes bug wide. "But it's not what you think. I wish I could tell you, but it's a secret."

Troy looked at me like I had lost my mind. "Okay, well...," he said slowly. "That's it then?"

"For now. Have a great day!"

I left Troy standing there in the hallway, trying to make sense of the new and improved, much happier, high-on-pole-vaulting me.

CHAPTER 26

It was my idea to get out the Christmas lights and to do everything we've always done as a family. We set up the tree and hung everybody's stocking, even Alex's. Mom and Grandma baked cookies and decorated them with frosting, like always. With Alex not there to eat any of the goodies, I had to slap my own hand to keep from pigging out on them.

Christmas Eve day was a Saturday, so I put on two layers of sweat clothes and two pairs of socks before going out to the loft. I bundled up in my heavy chore coat and walked across the snow-packed yard. It was the coldest day of the year so far. I wasn't sure how much pole-vaulting I could do dressed in so many layers, but I was determined to try.

I stomped the snow off my shoes and climbed up the ladder. "Good afternoon, Alex! Merry Christmas!"

"Merry Christmas to you! Gosh, it looks like you've gained ten pounds since I saw you last," he said. "Have you been eating all my cookies?"

"I'm wearing two pairs of sweat clothes, goof ball. Do you think I can vault with all this on? I feel like a mummy."

"Well, why don't you go through your regular warm-up and we'll see what you can do."

I blew into my hands. Even with gloves on, my fingers were getting numb. "Wait a minute! I've got an idea," I said. "I'll be right back. Stay where you are."

"Like I was going anyplace?"

I climbed down the ladder to the first floor of the barn and walked across to the stalls where we had kept sheep. There was a metal lamp clamped to the stall. It has a bulb that generates a lot of heat, for baby livestock. I took the lamp back up the ladder, clamped the lamp onto the wall, plugged it in, and turned it on. I took off my gloves and warmed my hands under its glow.

I grabbed my pole and tried a few warm-up runs. The extra clothes slowed me down a lot, and I couldn't vault with gloves on.

"How about some short-approach jumps today?" Alex said. "You don't have to run as far or as fast, and you'll get a lot of good work done."

I jumped about twenty times from four steps, making six feet time after time. When I missed, which wasn't often, it was usually because I'd forgotten to get my alignment correct, leaned back at the takeoff, or didn't get enough speed into the jump.

Every three or four vaults, my fingers would go numb. I'd thaw them out under the lamp where some of the cats had curled up in the warm straw. As cold as it was up there, I don't think I could have vaulted without that lamp to warm up my hands.

After less than an hour, Alex said it was time to call it a day.

"We're debating whether to go to Christmas Eve services tonight," I said, putting my heavy coat back on.

"Christmas is a good thing. Peace on Earth, good will toward men. Tidings of great joy. Kept in the proper perspective, those are good and truthful messages."

"What does that mean? Should we go or not?" I really didn't want to because it would be the first time we'd been to church since before... you know.

"The Spirit of the universe is everywhere present, so the message of Christmas is true every day and not just at Christmas time. The story of baby Jesus is a story of new birth. Of hope. It's worth remembering. I think you should go and see for yourself."

"But it's always the same."

"This year you might be surprised with what you discover. I'll go with you if you want."

"You're always with me."

"Touché! That's true. Save me a seat?"

We pulled into the church parking lot just before seven. It was snowing. There were several rows of pickup trucks and cars parked in the lot. The little sanctuary was going to be full.

Electric candles flickered in every window. Wreaths hung on the red doors. Dad held the door open as we entered the foyer, which was decorated like it always was for Christmas. "Let's sit in the back," I said.

We took our programs from the usher, who seemed glad to see us. The bulletin had a photo of a poinsettia on it, the official flower of Christmas. I spied four seats on the back row and went over and sat down. A few people gawked at us but most people didn't turn around—just how I wanted it. I wiggled out of my coat. The sanctuary was lit by the glow of real candles. It was time for the service to begin.

Rev. Stark began to read from the Bible: "And he shall be called…"

I remembered what Alex had said about the true, deeper meaning of Christmas. I felt comforted by familiar surroundings, the memories of so many past Christmas Eves.

We sang lots of carols, including "Hark the Herald Angels Sing." I felt like the music was reaching me in some inner place. I felt in harmony, not only with the people in this sanctuary but with people all around the world who were singing these same songs in different languages. I felt a lump in my throat.

I thought about the deep conversations Grandma and I had had. She'd said, "God is fully present, is everywhere all the time." I felt that presence as we sang. It was just like Alex had said: "You might be surprised with what you discover." Tears rolled down my cheeks.

I closed my eyes. I could see Alex's face. I could hear him singing. We got up right after the service was over, but Reverend and Mrs. Stark and Scott were already greeting people at the door. I just smiled and said, "Merry Christmas."

CHAPTER 27

On the Monday after holiday break the principal read the following announcement over the school intercom:

"Welcome back to Grain Valley High School, and happy new year to all you Threshers! The basketball team will be traveling to Erie tomorrow. The bus will leave promptly at two p.m. We will host Cherryvale on Friday. The representative from the U.S. Army will be on campus Wednesday to meet with seniors interested in enlisting after graduation. Congratulations to Troy Timmerman for being named to the Class 3A All-State football team. Believe it or not, it's time for you seniors to get measured for your caps and gowns. A representative will be here on Thursday to take your measurements and a $25 deposit. The deposit is nonrefundable, so buckle down and don't flunk out, okay?"

I felt the hair go up on the back of my neck, like I was on top of the big hill on a roller coaster, about to plunge. I knew I was going to pass all my classes. I was going to graduate, but I had no idea what I was going to do after I took off my cap and gown.

I saw Big Troy in the hall between classes. "Congratulations!" I said.

He looked down at me and smiled. "Thanks, Maggie. It feels pretty good, considering what a lousy season we had."

I felt a tingle as he put his giant hands on top of mine. He had nice dimples when he smiled and sparkling hazel eyes with lovely long eyelashes. We'd been friends forever, but I'd never noticed him like that—until now.

We stood there looking at each other as the crowd of students passed by. He didn't let go of my hands, and I didn't mind.

A scrawny freshman reached up and punched Troy on the shoulder. "Way to go, Big Troy!" he squeaked. "You rock!"

"Thanks, kid," Troy replied. But our eyes stayed fixed on each other a moment longer before he let go of my hands. My heart pounded and I felt weak in the knees.

"Um, hey," he said, "do you think you'd like to go out with me some-time? Like on a date?"

I flushed. "Sure. I mean, I'd like that."

"Are you free on Saturday? We could go over to Fort Scott, get something to eat and then see a movie?"

"Saturday? Let me check my appointment calendar," I said. "I think I can squeeze you in."

"Awesome! Pick you up around five?"

I couldn't stop smiling. I nodded up at his smiling face, thinking, *Who is this handsome young man, and where has he been all my life?*

"Maggie?"

"Huh?"

"Five o'clock?"

"Sure, great. It's a date!"

The bell sounded. We were both late for our next class.

"Shoot! Gotta go!"

I watched him run down the hall. There wasn't a pound of fat on him. I turned and walked to my ag class. "Oops!" I said as I went in the door. Mr. Williams was taking roll.

"Miss Steele, thank you for joining us. Take your seat."

"Glad to be here!" I said. I could still feel Troy's eyes looking at me. I smiled and kept smiling the rest of the day.

At supper I told Mom and Dad about the cap and gown and needing $25 for a deposit. I also said that the army recruiter was coming. Dad stopped moving his fork toward his open mouth, closed his mouth with a clack of his teeth, and looked at me steadily.

"I'm not going into the military, don't worry."

"Don't even talk to them, okay, honey?" Mom said.

"I won't, I won't. Gosh, forget I said anything."

Dad opened his mouth and inserted a bite of mashed potatoes and gravy. Message sent.

"And, oh, Big Troy made the all-state team," I said casually.

"Good for him," Dad said. "He deserves it. He has worked hard. He has a Division I body."

I choked on my milk. "What?" I sputtered.

"He's big enough and athletic enough to pass the off-the-bus test."

I looked at him blankly.

"Lots of high school football players think they're good enough to play major college football, but they've no idea how big and strong those players are at Kansas or Kansas State. Coaches know how big a player needs to be. They can tell as soon as he gets off the bus if he's big enough for big-time football." Dad put another helping of food on his plate and raised his fork. "Some players are big enough, but they aren't really athletic enough. They dominated in high school because they were bigger than everyone else, but in the Big 12, all of the players are giants. But Big Troy has made himself into a real prospect."

I laughed at Dad's scouting report. I'd been thinking the exact same thing, but for a totally different reason. "Um, well, Troy kind of invited me out on a date Saturday, for dinner and a movie, and I said yes." I hid my smile behind my glass of milk.

Mom and Dad exchanged some sort of coded message in their glance.

"That's nice, dear," Mom said.

Dad nodded, shoveling in a bite of pot roast. "I think Troy could play at a big school. Is he still sold on Emporia State?"

"I think so. I don't know," I said. *But I think he's sold on me!*

I helped Mom clear the table and do the dishes.

"Well, do you like him?" she asked, handing me a plate.

"As a friend," I said, drying it and putting it in the cupboard. I thought about our hands and his eyes and his dimples and the look on his handsome face. "I've never really noticed him before, until today."

Mom pulled the stopper out of the soapy water and the pipes gurgled as the water went down the drain. "What does he plan to do with himself?" she asked. "What does he want to study at college? I mean, is he smart?"

"Yes, he's smart, and he's funny. And he carries himself well, considering that he's the best athlete at Grain Valley. What I mean is, he's not big-headed."

We walked out of the kitchen toward the living room where Dad was watching TV.

"Let's not get carried away here, okay?" I said. "It's not like we're dating, it's just a date."

Mom smiled. "Of course, dear, just go out and have a good time. You deserve it. It's your senior year." Thanks for reminding me, I thought. "No TV for me. I've got homework; calculus and science."

"Good night, then," Mom said.

"'Night."

It was after eleven when I finally got done with my homework. I found my mind wandering, thinking about Troy. I've never been boy-crazy. I mean, Caleb and I had never been all that serious, not like Alex and Betsy or so many other couples at Grain Valley. I'd never felt this way before, which was a good thing, I think. Who needs all that drama? Going ga-ga over a guy, then breaking up and going out with some other guy. There were girls in my class who'd dated just about every guy in school, if you know what I mean. I guess I've been too busy or something.

It was too late to pole-vault, but I still needed to talk to Alex. I went through the kitchen and pulled on my chore coat. The ground was frozen solid. A heavy layer of clouds hung low overhead. It felt like it could start snowing any minute. It was even too cold for the cats.

The loft was as cold as a freezer. I flipped on the lights. "Hello? Is anybody here?"

I turned on the heat lamp and stood under it. Wind whined through the rafters. There was a long silence.

"Alex? Are you here?"

"Sorry, Sis, I was in Australia, vacationing in the outback."

"Very funny."

"Seriously, it's summer there this time of year."

"That sounds nice." I could see my breath. "Wait a minute! You mean you can go anywhere you like?"

"Absolutely, anywhere I want. You think I just hang around up here, waiting for you to show up? That's not how it works, you know."

"No, I don't know how it works. In fact, I still have a million questions about how it works where you are."

"Ask away."

"Well," I said, "what about the other people who've died—are they with you where you are?"

"We use the words 'crossed over' or 'made the final transition.' 'Died' sounds too permanent, like it's the end, which it isn't. Getting here is just a new beginning. But yes, everybody's here. It's a wonderful, marvelous thing."

"What about Caleb? Is he there with you? Can Betsy hear him? Can Betsy hear you?"

"I've seen Caleb around. Betsy hasn't been looking for us here. She visits our graves. She thinks we're still in the ground. It's pretty sad, really."

I sat down on the bale of straw under the heat lamp. "Did you see what happened today? At school, I mean?"

"Of course I saw. I think you and Troy would make a nice couple."

I felt my cheeks flush with embarrassment. Talk about awkward! "Hey," I said suddenly, "can you read my thoughts? Do you know what I'm thinking? Because that would be creepy. An invasion of privacy!"

"Relax. Give me some credit. It doesn't work that way. I'm just saying that from my perspective, you and Troy seem right for each other. It's all good. You've been friends, now you can be better friends, in a relationship based on friendship, not on some fantasy."

I realized that I'd been fantasizing about Troy. "Are you sure you haven't been reading my mind?"

"Cross my heart and hope to die!"

"You're already dead, silly," I laughed.

"And you've never felt more alive than you've been feeling lately, with the vaulting and the new boyfriend thing."

"He's not my boyfriend!"

"Whatever. Hey, it's getting late and it's cold up here. You really oughtta turn in."

"Yes, it is, late and cold!" I couldn't feel my feet. I stomped them a few times as I stood up to click off the heat lamp. I walked over to the ladder, stomping the numbness out of them. "Good night, Alex."

"G'day, mate," he said in an Aussie accent.

I dreamed that Troy and I were walking across the high school stage in our caps and gowns. Then the announcer said, "Welcome to the Bill Snyder Family Stadium, home of the Kansas State Wildcats!" There was a big roar from the crowd, and I was in it. We were all dressed in purple. It was the strangest dream, but when I woke up the next morning, it seemed like it had been real.

CHAPTER 28

The doorbell rang at 4:55 Saturday afternoon. Troy had been parked down the road since 4:45. I knew this because Dad had stopped to see if he'd broken down and needed help.

"Troy is parked and waiting down the road," Dad said.

I was in the bathroom, trying to decide how much makeup I should put on and what to do with my hair. I was thinking about pulling it back and tying it with a red ribbon, which looked cute. But did I want cute, or something else?

"What's he wearing?" I asked.

"Don't know. Aftershave for sure, definitely aftershave." Dad laughed. "He's got gel in his hair, looks as nervous as I've ever seen him. He jumped when I honked, and when he saw it was me all the color ran out of his face. Come to think of it, I think he was wearing a button-down shirt and a blue sweater."

I felt my hands get clammy and my mouth went dry. I hadn't expected to feel so much pressure. I'd already spent an hour trying on different clothes. I'd settled on jeans and a red-print snap-button blouse with my rhinestone belt and new leather boots.

"You look beautiful, dear," Mom said, folding my shirt collar and patting me on the shoulders. She stood behind me. We were looking at each other in the bathroom mirror when the doorbell rang.

"He's here!" I said, fumbling with the ribbon. I thought about yanking it out but changed my mind. He put gel in his hair, I thought. I'll leave the ribbon in mine.

Troy was in the living room. He looked happy to see me. "You look good," he said.

"Thanks, so do you." He smelled good, too.

Mom and Dad stood there. Frost was fogging up the storm door. It was cold outside.

"Well, we'd better get going," Troy said. I had my heavy coat in my hands. He reached out to take it from me. I glanced at Mom and bugged my eyes. Nobody had helped me with my coat since I was about three. He patted me gently, like I was wearing shoulder pads.

"See you later!" I called, as I went out the door he held open for me. He opened the door of his truck too, making sure I was seated before shutting the door. He'd left the truck running. It was toasty and warm. Some country music was playing on his stereo. I liked what I was experiencing.

We ate at the Sirloin Stockade, the nicest place to eat in Fort Scott. We ate big salads and steak, baked potatoes with sour cream, and warm cinnamon rolls. Troy ate two steaks and two baked potatoes. He asked lots of questions about me—what music I liked to listen to, what I liked to eat, when my birthday was, all sorts of things. Then he asked, "What are you going to do after graduation?"

"I have no idea," I said.

"Why?"

"Because with my brother gone, there's nobody left to take over our farm, except me."

"Why wouldn't you want to keep it going?"

"Lots of reasons."

"It seems like paradise out there to me."

"It is and it isn't." I put down my steak knife and fork. How to explain? Troy leaned his broad shoulders forward, his hazel eyes filled with concern. "It's kind of a touchy subject," I said, bailing. He didn't ask anything else about it. "What about you, what are your plans?" I really wanted to know.

Even though we'd been classmates and friends for a long time, we had never talked that much. I didn't know he lived in town, or that his dad was the city administrator, whatever that was, or that his mom was a teller at the bank. I found out he had an older sister who was married to a firefighter in Salina. He was the tallest person in his family, naturally, and his grandfather was a giant of a man.

We both had ice cream sundaes for dessert. There were a lot of people in the restaurant, but we were the only teenage couple. The waitress asked if we wanted coffee, and when Troy said yes, I said okay too, and poured in lots of sugar, which made him laugh.

"I always like a little coffee with my sugar," I said.

"I can see that," he laughed.

A man I didn't know came up and said, "Congratulations on a fine high school career!"

Troy shook the man's hand and said, "Thank you, sir." As the man walked away, Troy whispered, "I have no idea who that was."

"The price of being famous."

"I'm hardly famous," he said. "Small-town hero, maybe."

"Dad says you're big enough and athletic enough to play Big 12 football. Are you still going to Emporia State?"

"That's the plan for now. They've offered me a scholarship. They have a good biology department. I'm going pre-med."

"You want to be a doctor?"

"A neurologist, a doctor who specializes in the nervous system. I want to help people who have Alzheimer's and Parkinson's disease. My mom has Parkinson's." He frowned.

"Is she—I mean, will she be all right?"

"Well, no. There is no cure, at least not yet. But the research looks promising." His eyes brightened and he raised his eyebrows, but he didn't smile. "But hey, let's not talk about that anymore, we're on our first date!"

"Our *first* date? You mean you think there's going to be more?"

He laughed and smiled again. "Hopefully! I mean, if you want."

I put my coffee cup to my lips, smiling. It tasted sweet.

The movie wasn't great, but who cares, right? I wound up leaning on his shoulder, which was big as a pillow. I put my hand on his massive arm, and he put his big hand over mine. It felt good and right. We held hands as he drove me home. He walked me to the front door, and asked if he could kiss me good night.

Let's just say it was the best part of the evening.

Mom came into my room wearing her robe. "Well?" she asked. "How did it go?"

I was still buzzing. "Great! He's great! He wants to be a doctor." And, I thought, *he kissed me! I can't feel my toes!*

"Your father thinks a lot of Troy. Alex liked him, too."

"I know he does. I mean, I know he did," I said, covering my slip-up. "Night, Mom."

"Good night, Maggie."

My mind was racing. I liked him, a lot! And he liked me! He'd asked me out again, to the Valentine's Day dance, hadn't he? And I didn't have to say yes. *Maggie,* I thought, *you might wind up marrying this guy, Dr. Troy Timmerman. Oh, shut up,* I said to myself with a laugh. *We're not even a couple, yet.*

It would've been easy to spend all of my time thinking about Troy and daydreaming about a possible future together. But my life went on pretty much the same after that. We ate lunch together at the cafeteria, which was different, and we walked together to class, which was different, and we waited for each other after school and walked together to the parking lot where our trucks were now parked side by side, which was different. But beyond that, things were pretty much the same.

CHAPTER 29

The weather was warming up a little. Instead of being as cold as twenty degrees, it was thirty or forty in the loft. I was vaulting up there almost every day. I'd also started lifting Alex's old weights and doing lots of rope climbing. I could climb almost all the way to the top without using my legs. It was hard at first, but now I was stronger than I'd ever been.

Alex cut me no slack. He had me do lots of sit-ups and push-ups—on my fingertips. The best part about getting stronger was that as the crossbar kept going up, I kept vaulting over it.

I was making seven feet from four steps in mid-January. I jumped eight feet running from six steps in early February. I recorded my progress on the old blackboard I'd used to record sheep stuff on. After I made a new personal record, or PR, I chalked it up on the board.

The Valentine's Day Dance was on a Friday, after the basketball game. Troy wore a nice suit. I wore a new red dress. The dance was held in the commons area, which had been decorated by the student council. We had our picture taken together under a big heart made of red and white balloons. There was a disc jockey who played too much rap music, which is impossible to dance to. Finally he played some country songs and we had a good time line-dancing. Troy took me straight home afterward because he had to get up early. Coach Snyder had invited him to visit K State!

"Can you see me in purple?" Troy asked. I smiled and kissed him good night.

The weather was mild and the moon was full, so I changed into one layer of sweats and headed for the loft. I climbed the ladder and shouted, "Hey! Let's vault!" I really wanted to see how high I could jump in just a single layer of sweat clothes.

"Hey, Sis! Why don't we have a make-believe competition, just like a real meet? That way you'll be ready when the real track season begins at the end of next month."

I stopped stretching my hamstrings. "What?"

"You're going out for the track team. They need a girl pole-vaulter. Tryouts are March 15th, which is just a month away. And close your mouth. You look like a catfish."

My jaw clomped shut with a clack. "You're joking, right?" I said. "I mean, you can't be serious. I've never run track before in my life!"

"What do you think you've been doing up here all winter? Of course you're going out for track. You're Grain Valley's best and only girl pole-vaulter."

"You really think I could do it?"

"You can do anything you want, Maggie. That's what I've been saying." Alex made his voice sound like he was talking on a loudspeaker. "Now vaulting (vaulting) for Grain Valley (Valley). At seven feet, six inches, Maggie! (Maggie!) Steele! (Steele!)"

A jolt of excitement shot through me. "Vaulters get three attempts at each height," he said. "After they call your name to make an attempt, you'll have one and a half minutes. That's just enough time to set your standards and get to your takeoff spot. When you get there, just relax but stay aggressive, which is the hardest thing to do in sports. Don't try to start your run too hard, too fast. Don't think you have to do anything different. Keep it the same, just like you practiced."

I did everything, just like he said, and soared way over seven-six.

"Great start!" Alex said. "Let's go up!"

I raised the bar to eight feet, stepping up on a hay bale on each side of the standards.

"Steele up!" said Alex the announcer.

I went through the same routine, with the same results.

"Excellent, Maggie. I think you're ready to try it from eight steps away now. And raise your top hand four inches."

I stepped further away than I'd ever run before, from almost underneath the basketball goal on the far end of the loft.

"A longer run will give you more speed with the same effort," Alex said. "It's not like you have to try harder, but with more speed you can hold higher and still carry into the pit safely." He switched to his announcer voice. "The bar is now at eight-six. Steele is up!"

I did just what Alex said, raising my hand on the pole four inches. I felt a jolt of nervous energy going through me. I took off down the runway, going faster than ever, but I knocked down the bar going over and landed on my back on the crossbar. It hurt. A lot.

I rolled around, holding my back. "That's going to leave a mark!"

"Welcome to the pole vault! You're a lucky girl, you know. You've been vaulting all this time with no bruises to show for it."

I struggled out of the pit. I took the crossbar to put it back up, but it was bent where I'd landed on it.

"Way to go!" Alex joked. "You bent the crossbar!"

Now I knew why it was so crooked.

By the time I got the bar straightened and back up on the standards, my back felt better, but it was still pretty sore.

"Steele's second attempt at eight feet six inches!"

I walked back to my new check mark and grabbed the pole at the higher handhold. I bent over to stretch my back, reaching the pole toward my shoes.

While I was working the kinks out, Alex said, "The good news is that you did everything right on that jump. You need to raise your grip an inch, and do it again, just like before."

I ran full speed, jumping high. It took longer to get up in the air but I went a lot higher. I landed hard on my back and felt my breath whoosh out of me.

I could hardly breathe, but I'd made it.

"Great vault! That's a new personal record for Maggie Steele!"

"I think I need more straw. A lot more straw!"

"Ladies (ladies) and gentlemen (gentlemen), there'll be a break in the action as we add more straw to the landing pit. Could we have some volunteers to the pole vault, please?"

"I'm guessing that would be me, right?" I got the pocketknife and cut the strings on five more bales. "That ought to do it!" I said, piling the straw really high. "I'm ready for nine feet!"

Alex was really getting into it. "Ladies (ladies) and gentlemen (gentlemen), the pole vault bar has been raised to nine feet, and there are only two vaulters left in the competition!"

"Two vaulters?"

"Maggie Steele from Grain Valley and What's Her Name from Another School."

"What's Her Name from Another School?" I asked.

"Of course! You didn't think they were just going to hand you a gold medal, did you?"

"But—"

"What's Her Name hasn't even started yet. She's been passing. She's so good she expects everybody else to go out before she even begins."

"Really? Well, that makes me mad!"

I flew down the runway, but something went wrong. I felt my shoulder jerk, and the pole stopped in mid-air. I rode the pole back down to the runway, and I landed hard on my feet. I really hurt my heels.

"That's a miss!"

"But I didn't knock the bar off!"

"But you went off the ground. When both feet go off the ground, it's a miss. Doesn't matter if you knock the bar off or not."

"Now you tell me!" I huffed.

"You have a minute or two to rest now because What's Her Name has decided to jump at this height after all."

"She can do that? I thought she was passing until I was done."

"Well, I guess she thinks you *are* done. And...What's Her Name has just made it, on her first try! Steele up, second attempt at nine feet. The clock is running."

I was really upset that What's Her Name had made it. I felt a jolt of competitive juice go through me as I stood at the end of the runway. I ran and planted my pole, determined to do all I could do to get over the bar. That willpower carried me up and over. I sank deep into the fresh straw.

"Yay, Maggie! I mean, that's Grain Valley's Maggie Steele (Steele) over nine feet in the pole vault. Still two contestants remaining."

My heart was burning to go even higher.

"What's Her Name has missed her first attempt at nine-six! Apparently she got rattled watching you make nine feet and lost her focus. Steele up! First attempt at nine-six!"

I ran down the runway and vaulted just as well as I had before, only I hit the bar with my left hip as I turned over. The bar wobbled and fell. I missed my last two tries the same way.

"Miss Steele, you are eliminated. But, congratulations, you got second place in your first meet!"

"Second place? But What's Her Name didn't make nine-six either. We both made nine feet. It's a tie!"

"Nope, sorry. In case of a tie, the winner is the vaulter with the fewest misses on the previous height. She made nine feet on her first try, but it took you two tries. Ergo, What's Her Name wins the gold medal."

"Poop!" I said, laughing.

It had been a fun make-believe track meet, and I had a new PR. I erased the eight feet from the blackboard and wrote nine feet in its place.

"I can't wait for track season!" I said, clapping the chalk dust off my hands.

CHAPTER 30

"How was your trip to Manhattan?" I asked Big Troy at school on the following Monday as we walked to class.

"Well, let's just say I have a big decision to make," he said, flashing his dimples. "Coach Snyder is an outstanding salesman. He wanted me to sign a letter of intent on the spot, but I didn't. I told him I needed to talk it over with my parents, and other important people in my life." He was looking straight at me. I felt myself blush.

"But what about Emporia State? Didn't you say you were going there?"

"I made a verbal commitment, but I didn't sign anything. I'm still free to choose. A full Division I scholarship from K State is a lot more money."

"How much?"

"They pay for everything, even the training table."

"Training table?"

"Food prepared especially for athletes. Emporia State is a Division II school. They can only give me tuition and books. I'd have to pay for everything else. That's the big difference. That, and the level of football."

I nodded. "Do you think you can play Big 12 Football?"

"You know, I'm surprised how confident Coach Snyder and his assistants are about me. They have game film of me from last season, blocking for your brother and Caleb. They like my footwork, which is important. And they said I can add another thirty pounds of muscle to my frame in their strength program."

"Can you see yourself playing in Bill Snyder Family Stadium?"

"It's funny. In the dorm, I dreamed I was playing football for K State. You were in the stands, dressed in purple, cheering for me. It was so real. I think it might be a sign. Do you believe in that sort of thing?"

Goose bump city. "I had a dream like that a few weeks ago!"

"You're kidding!"

"I'm totally serious."

We hugged right there in the hallway, which is against school rules—no PDA.

"See you at lunch," he said.

"It's a lunch date!"

Troy Timmerman is going to K-State! Dr. Troy Timmerman! Maggie Timmerman. Mrs. Maggie Timmerman. I found myself writing these words in my notebook in American history class. I covered them with my hand and looked to see if anyone was looking.

My doodling was interrupted by the principal's daily announcement. "Spring sports will begin practice four weeks from today. If you're planning to go out for softball, baseball, or track, you must have a physical exam and parental consent forms signed. Pick up the forms in Coach Wilson's office. The representative from Wichita State will be in the commons area today during lunch."

Wait a minute! I hadn't planned to tell my parents about me pole-vaulting, at least not yet. My mind raced. What if they refused to sign the slip?

I took in a deep breath and blew it out, ruffling Scott Stark's hair. He touched the back of his head and turned around, looking at me strangely.

I narrowed my eyebrows. "Sorry!" I whispered. "Just turn around."

"Miss Steele, Mr. Stark," the teacher said. "Do you have something to share with the class?"

"No ma'am, sorry," I said.

I wasn't ready to share with anyone, at least not yet. But it looked like the whole world was going to know about it soon enough.

I walked past Coach Wilson's office. The door was open, so I stepped inside. His chair was empty, but the physical exam forms and permission slips were on the desk. I took one of each and was putting them in my book bag—

"Hello, Maggie! Can I help you?"

Coach Wilson was standing in the doorway. He saw me putting the papers into my bag. Busted! "Oh, are you going out for softball?" he asked.

"Or something," I said, smiling. "I thought it would be fun to do some kind of sport before I leave high school. After all, this is my last chance!"

"Well, you look athletic enough. If you can make a varsity team, you can participate as a senior. The junior varsity teams are just for underclassmen, but you know that."

"Sure," I said, even though I didn't have a clue. "Well, thanks, Coach, gotta go!" I headed for the door.

"Oh, Maggie! Do you have a minute?"

"Sure, Coach, what's up?"

"I have a favor to ask you," he said. "My son Zackary has been begging me to bring him back out to your place, to play on that rope swing up in your barn. There's a half-day in-service for teachers and administrators this Friday. My wife teaches at the elementary, which means we'd normally send Zack to the baby-sitter's. But if you aren't too busy..."

"Sure, I'll watch him! I promised last summer I'd show him how to swing on the Tarzan rope. I'm surprised he remembered."

"Are you kidding? Not a week goes by that he doesn't talk about it. I'll call the principal at the grade school and tell him you'll pick Zack up at noon—if you're sure it's all right."

"Positive," I answered. "We'll have a great time!"

CHAPTER 31

On Friday, Zack sprinted out the front door of the grade school, looking for my truck. He wore a red Kansas City Chiefs jacket, a pair of leather work gloves just like in the summer, and had an adorable smile on his face.

"Hi, Maggie!"

"Hi, Zack! Great to see you! Can you put your seatbelt on?"

Zack talked nonstop on the way to the farm. "I wore my gloves to hang onto the rope with! Can we go up in the barn right away? How far is it to your farm? Have you had lunch yet? Because I already ate. But if you need to eat, I can wait until after dinner. Dad says I have to listen to everything you say. Have you been swinging on the rope this winter? Is it cold up there? Do you wear gloves on your hands? I'm sure I can rope swing! But will you help me? I mean, if I need a little boost or something?"

I let him ramble, nodding and smiling and laughing at his total enthusiasm. He was so excited.

I skipped lunch so Zack could go right up to the loft. He climbed the ladder with no fear whatsoever. I felt like a little girl again, going up to the Tarzan ropes with my brother. Zack ran to the hanging ropes. I thought about announcing the arrival of our special guest to Alex, but I didn't need to—I knew he could see him.

"This is the coolest place!" he said. "I wish I had a barn like this!"

"You can come here any time. How would you like to learn to swing on that rope?"

"I want to go really high!"

Where had I heard that before? "I knew a boy like you once. He was very brave. He could swing all the way across, from this ladder to that one."

"Cool! I want to do that!"

"Well, let's teach you to stand up on the rope first, then we'll talk about swinging." I showed Zack how to put his little feet on the big knot at the bottom of the rope.

Pushing on the Chiefs logo on the back of his jacket, I walked the rope a couple of steps away from center and let go.

Zack shouted. He was having the time of his life, and I was eight years old again. "Alex?" I asked in a whisper. "Are you watching this?"

"Just like old times!" he whispered back.

I pushed Zack back and forth across the loft, but he wanted to go higher still. "Let's you and me swing together," I suggested. "I'll get on first and you hang on to me."

I carried the rope to the ladder on the wall and climbed up to the first rung. "Okay, now you climb up here and face me."

He climbed, quick as a monkey, wrapped his legs around my waist, and held on tight. We swung back and forth like that until the rope was perfectly still.

I'd spent the moment remembering.

"Let's do it again!"

"Okay," I said, wiping my eyes with my sleeve.

"I want to try it by myself!"

I watched the little guy carry the rope to the ladder and climb all the way up to the top rung. He smiled a daring smile I'd seen so many times before.

"No way, buster!" I said.

Zack took one step down and looked at me. I shook my head. He stepped down another rung and jumped.

I felt a rush of panic because I'd forgotten to tell him how to keep from crashing into the wall. But before I could yell, he pushed away with both feet. He'd handled it a lot better than Scott Stark.

Zack swung several more times before he was ready for a time-out. "I'm thirsty," he said, so we went to the kitchen for a glass of milk and the chocolate-chip cookies I'd made the night before. He looked so cute, sitting in the same chair my brother always sat in.

"Can we do it again?" he asked. "I'm not tired!"

I laughed and said sure. He ran ahead and disappeared into the barn. By the time I got there Zack had already climbed the ladder.

"Wow! What's this? A pole jumping thing?"

I climbed up to see what he was doing. He was holding my vaulting pole in his little leather-gloved hands. He ran around, pushing the pole. It was way too long for him.

"Can *you* do this?" he asked.

"A little."

"Show me! Pleeease?"

Alex whispered, "I think that's a great idea! You'd be a great coach."

"I don't know if your parents would approve of you pole-vaulting," I said. I still didn't know if *my* parents would approve of *me* pole-vaulting.

I was still wearing the clothes I'd worn to school, with running shoes instead of boots. "All right," I said. "But promise you won't tell anyone. It has to be our little secret, okay?"

He looked at me blankly. "Sure, I won't tell."

I put the bar at seven feet. "You can go that high?" he said in amazement.

"Well, we'll see," I said, taking my pole to my six-step mark on the floor. I gripped about two feet lower than usual, took a breath, and half-ran, half-jogged to the box, planted the pole, and swung neatly over the bar.

"WOW!" Zack shouted.

I laughed. "You're the only living person who has ever seen me do that."

"Can you go higher than that?"

"Let's see," I said.

I jumped over seven-six easily. Zack cheered like I'd won the Olympics.

"Higher!" he shouted. I put the bar at eight feet, which was almost as high as I'd ever gone from six steps.

Alex whispered, "Don't look now, but you've got company."

Dad and Coach Wilson had snuck into the loft. They were standing by the ladder.

"Well, the cat's out of the bag now," Alex said. "Might as well show them what you've been doing up here."

I felt an incredible surge of energy—vaulting for an audience! I took a deep breath and let it out. I ran six progressively faster steps, hitting my plant perfectly. I cleared the bar easily.

"Yippee!" Zack shouted. "You made it! Eight feet!"

I heard the muffled sound of gloved hands clapping as I got out of the straw. I picked up my pole and waved as the men walked toward me.

"What's going on here?" Dad said, surprised but happy.

"Well...we've been—I mean, I've been teaching myself to pole-vault. A little." I walked over and picked up *Track and Field for Boys,* opened it to page seventy-four, and handed it to my dad.

"You taught yourself to pole-vault with this book?" Dad asked.

"That's about it," I said.

"Isn't she great, Dad?" Zack shouted. "Isn't she great?"

Coach Wilson didn't know what to say. He just stood there looking at me, scratching his head. "I've never seen anything like it!" he said at last, with a broad smile.

I smiled back at him. "I can jump higher from a longer run, when I'm wearing sweats, you know. I was just playing around."

"Playing around?" he said. "Young lady, you may think you were just playing around, but eight feet would've been high enough to score points at last year's league meet! We've never had a girl pole-vaulter at our school."

I showed them the blackboard with my PRs on it, explaining how we'd been practicing from short approaches and long approaches, and about our strength workouts and everything. Only I had to make sure that I said it like I'd been doing it all by myself. I was talking nonstop. I could see them staring at me, not knowing whether to believe any of it.

"Let me see if I understand this," said Coach Wilson. "You've vaulted nine feet, here, in this barn?"

"I'm about to make nine-six," I said. "We—I have a few things to work out before I can go as high as I want."

"How high do you want to go?" Zack asked.

I looked at his happy, hopeful face and said, "Over the moon, buddy. Over the moon!"

"Wow! That would be cool!"

"So this explains your visit to my office to get the permission forms," Coach said. "You're coming out for track, right?"

I looked at Dad, asking him the big question with my eyes. He nodded and smiled. "I guess so," I said. "I mean, if you think it's all right."

Coach looked at me like I was joking, but I wasn't. He slapped Dad on the back and laughed. "I'm sure Coach Dillinger will be overjoyed to see you at tryouts!"

In the meantime, Zack had taken a rope three steps high on the wall ladder. "Hey, Daddy, watch this!" he shouted, before launching himself across the barn.

"Ohmygosh!" Coach Wilson exclaimed.

"He's a great little athlete," I said. Zack was having the time of his life.

"You people are remarkable," Coach said. "And this—this is an amazing place."

"Coach, you have no idea," I said. "And Zack's welcome to come back here any time."

Coach smiled. "I have a feeling we're going to remember this for the rest of our lives."

CHAPTER 32

Dad and I kept the secret from Mom, at least until supper.

"Well, that was quite an exciting time we had in the loft this afternoon," he said, eyeing me suggestively. *Tell her!*

"Yes!" I said, sipping my milk. "Zack really took to that rope swing, didn't he?" *No!*

"Coach Wilson was really excited about *all* of the athletic talent he saw up there, wasn't he?" *Tell her!*

"Yes, his *son* is going to a real star." *No!*

Mom looked at Dad. Dad nodded at me.

"What's going on?" she asked.

"Oh, nothing," I said.

Dad laughed and pointed at me. "You tell her or I will."

I reached for my milk and held the glass to my mouth, giggling.

"Margaret Ann! What is going on?" Mom demanded.

"Maggie has a big secret," Dad said. My heart dropped into my stomach. Did he know? "She's been pole-vaulting, up in the barn," he added excitedly, spilling half the beans.

"What?" Mom asked.

"She set up the old standards and taught herself to pole-vault—from a book!"

"A book?"

"That's exactly what I said, but I saw her myself. She's really good!"

"At pole vaulting?" Mom blinked at Dad and at me. "But I thought pole vaulting was just for boys."

"It used to be," Dad said. "But nowadays girls do it too. Coach Wilson was real excited, wasn't he, Maggie?"

I nodded but kept quiet, still waiting to hear what Mom had to say.

"But can't you get hurt pole-vaulting? Isn't it really dangerous?"

"Well, I've landed on the crossbar a few times, and that really smarts," I said. "But it's not nearly as dangerous as hang gliding or sky-diving or doing back flips on a motorcycle. I don't think it's even as dangerous as swinging from one side of the loft to the other on the rope swing, and I've been doing that since I was what, eight years old?"

Mom looked skeptical. Dad weighed in. "It looks pretty safe to me," he said. "She has the biggest pile of straw to land in I've ever seen."

Mom chewed without speaking. Dad and I exchanged glances. He made an expression that said, *Just give her a minute to get her head around what she's just heard. It'll be fine, trust me.* But Mom didn't say another word at the table, and she stayed tight-lipped as we washed the dishes.

I took the permission slip, laid it on the table, and went to bed. When I got up the next morning, the permission slip had been signed, by both of them. I held the paper up to show it to Alex and spun around in a happy little circle. I was in!

After a week of doubly intense workouts, I cleared nine-six. And Mom and Dad were there to see it. Mom said, "You look so graceful on that pole. It's a beautiful thing to watch. I'm *so* proud of you, and I think Alex would be proud of you, too!"

"Oh, I know he is," I said. "I mean, I'm sure he was. I mean...hey, I'm hungry. Let's eat!"

I passed my physical and turned in my paperwork to Coach Wilson, who seemed delighted to see me in his office.

"How's it going?" he said.

"Oh, fine, just fine. I made nine-six."

"Nine-six?" He took a three-ring binder off the bookshelf and opened it. "Nine-six would have placed second at last year's league meet, which was won with a vault of ten-six." He was smiling at me, looking a little goofy. "Truth be told, we've only had a handful of *boys* who could vault nine-six. The boys' school record is twelve feet. We haven't had anyone close to that for a long time. Pole vaulting is hard to learn without good coaching, and good pole vault coaches are mighty hard to find."

I have a really good pole vaulting coach, I thought. *In fact, my coach is out of this world!*

Coach Wilson saw me grinning. He took it as a sign that he should keep talking. "There are a few younger boys who might come out and fool around with it some, but Scott will be the only boy varsity pole-vaulter this season."

I blinked. "Scott Stark?"

Coach nodded and kept talking, but I don't remember another word he said.

I talked to myself all the way down the hallway, stewing. *Scott Stark!? A pole-vaulter? Who knew?* My mind went back to all of the conflicts we'd had since, like, forever. And now we were going to be doing the same event? No way!

I climbed the ladder to the loft, still fuming. "Hey, Alex, guess what?"

"Scott's going to be your teammate? How ever did I know?"

"It's not one bit funny."

"But it is painfully ironic, right?"

"Whatever. I have a bad feeling about it. He's such a smart aleck. What will he say about me pole-vaulting?"

"What can he say? You're a pole-vaulter who happens to be a girl, end of story. Let him say whatever he wants."

"But what if he starts asking me a bunch of questions? Like how I learned to pole-vault? Dad and Mom and Coach Wilson believe I taught myself from a book. What will Coach Dillinger think? He's a track coach. Do you think he will believe that a girl who's never been out for any sport could teach this to herself?"

"What do you think Scott'll do when you show how good you are?"

"I think Scott'll pee his pants!"

"Then that should be all the motivation you need to vault well at tryouts. Which reminds me, you need to bring a measuring tape up here, along with a notebook and a pencil. You'll need to write down your check mark and move it to the runway at the stadium. It should be about the same, depending on the wind."

"I've never vaulted outside before," I said, feeling worried.

"Dad has a fifty-foot measuring tape. He'll be glad to help. Of course, you'll need to ask Scott to help you with your check marks once you get to school."

"I'd rather do it myself."

"I know, but there's a code among vaulters. They always help each other."

"Oh, gag me!"

There was something else I wanted to ask Alex. It was really important, but I was afraid to find out the answer. I finally got up my nerve. "Hey, will you be there, at the tryout?"

"I'll always be with you," he said. "You know that."

"No, I mean, will you be able to coach me? Will I still be able to hear you, like I can up here?"

"Of course!"

I felt a huge weight lift from my shoulders. "That's the best news I've heard all day!" I said, because it was.

CHAPTER 33

On Monday the principal made the following announcement: "Congratulations to Troy Timmerman, who signed a letter of intent to play football at Kansas State University! Troy's the first Thresher to receive a football scholarship from a D-I school. We'll be cheering for you next fall!

"Tryouts for the track teams will be held tomorrow after school at the stadium. You must have your forms turned in to participate. Runners will be timed in the 100-, 400-, and 1500-meter runs. Field event tryouts will be held for the discus, shot put, javelin, high jump, triple jump, and pole vault. See Coach Dillinger for details. The representative from the University of Kansas will be on campus Thursday."

I was excited and ready and nervous and scared, all at the same time. I kept wondering what it would be like to vault outside.

I heard the class laughing. Scott snapped his fingers in my face.

"Huh?" I said.

"Wake up, Maggie! Mr. Sherman asked you a question."

I was daydreaming in calculus, which was always dangerous with Mr. Sherman. He was the strictest teacher in the whole school.

"I'm sorry, could you repeat that?" I asked, coming back from la-la land.

"Never mind, Miss Steele," Mr. Sherman said. "That will cost you five points off your participation grade."

"But Mr. Sherman, I know the answer!" I couldn't afford to lose five points.

"Miss Steele, I beg to differ. You don't even know the question."

The room was as quiet as a tomb. Then Scott laughed. I kicked his desk. I felt like the mummy or the dummy, one of the two.

After supper I went to the hayloft with Dad. We measured my mark from six and eight steps, along with the midpoint check mark, which was four left footsteps from my takeoff. I wrote them down in a little notebook. Dad helped me get my vaulting pole down the ladder and tied it to the passenger side of my pickup with baling twine.

The following morning, I was too nervous to eat breakfast. I had to scrape frost off the windshield of my truck. I kept an eye on my pole all the way to school, but it stayed on just fine.

Troy was leaning on his truck, waiting for me. "You're late." he said, tapping his watch. "We're going to be tardy."

I laughed. "Tardy? I haven't heard that word in a long time."

"What's this?" Troy asked, pointing at my pole.

"Oh, that's my pole vaulting pole. I'm going out for the track team. Tryouts are this afternoon."

"You're kidding, right?"

I gave him a look that I doubt he'd seen from me before.

"You're seriously going to try to pole-vault with that thing?"

"That *thing* is an authentic bamboo pole from the golden age of sports. I've been practicing. You should come out to watch. You might be surprised."

Troy held up both hands, calling a truce. "Hey, I'll be out there anyway. I'm the best shot-putter on the team."

We walked into school, holding hands. "You're full of surprises, Maggie Steele," he said.

"And you're just full of it, Troy Timmerman." I gave him a kiss on the cheek and headed for class.

Troy called after me, "I love you!"

I turned around. "I bet you say that to all of your pole-vaulting girlfriends!" Our eyes met. Was this really happening? YES!

After the longest school day of my life, the last bell finally rang. I went out and sat on the bleachers wearing two layers of sweat clothes and my chore jacket because it was very cold and windy outside. Coach Dillinger blew his whistle at 3:30 sharp.

"Today we're conducting tryouts for the Grain Valley track team. If you're here to try out for softball or baseball, you're in the wrong place." Everybody laughed. "It's a little chilly, so my advice is to bundle up and stay tough!"

Coach Dillinger was definitely old-school. I wondered how he'd react to a girl pole-vaulter. I was about to find out. "If you're trying out for a jumping event, line up when your name is called."

I got up from my seat in the bleachers. I stood behind Scott Stark, as usual.

"What are *you* doing here?" he asked.

"Trying out for track," I said bluntly.

"What event?"

"Pole vault."

He laughed and laughed.

"Hey! Settle down back there!" Coach Dillinger said. "Now, you seniors who've done your events before will be in charge of the tryout at your event. You have exactly ten minutes to get your gear and get out there. Let's move it, people!"

I was hot and sweaty from wearing two layers of sweats inside the overheated gym, and from being so nervous. I pulled on my leather gloves and a head warmer, and headed out into the cold.

"We don't have any poles for girls," Scott said. "But I guess you can use mine."

I'd left my pole outside. I picked it up and walked to the track.

"What's that?" Scott asked.

"My pole vaulting pole."

"Looks like a fishing pole."

"Well, it isn't."

"My pole's in the equipment room. We need to get the crossbar, too. The standards should be out there."

I waited as Scott went into the equipment room under the stadium. He came out with a yellow crossbar and a white vaulting pole.

I followed him across the football field to the pole vault pit, which looked very different than the straw pile back home. I called under my breath, my voice hidden in the wind, "Hey, Alex, you out here?"

"Right here!" he answered. "You ready to do some vaulting?"

"Right now I'm so nervous, I can barely breathe. And it's freezing out here!"

"You'll be fine. You need to mark your step. Ask Scott to help."

"No!" I shouted. Scott turned around. I smiled nervously. He smiled back at me.

The pole vault mat was covered by a gold cover, like for a tent or something. "We have to take the cover off the pit first," Scott said. "I could use some help unfastening the latches." He plopped down on the edge of the pit and unfastened a hook. "Like this," he said as he unlatched the next one. There were a lot of latches holding down the cover. I sat down on the mat but couldn't get my latch undone.

"You have to bounce really hard on it," he said, sitting way too close to me.

It took a while, but I got the hang of it. I was confused about why we needed to take the cover off, but I didn't say anything.

"Now we set up the standards," he said. He pointed to a long metal bar that looked like the one in my barn. "You take that end." I grabbed my end, expecting it to be heavy, but it was surprisingly light. We struggled to get the standards in place in the gusty wind, but eventually we did get them up there.

"I could use some help getting my measurements," I said finally.

Scott looked at me like I was from Mars. "You have *measurements*?"

"A few. I mean, yes." I pulled the little notebook out of my gym bag, along with the measuring tape.

"How can you already have measurements if you've never vaulted before?"

"Who says I haven't?"

I handed Scott the front end of the tape and started spooling it out, walking down the runway. He went to the back of the box and laid down the tape, which flapped wildly in the wind. I marked my step with a piece of chalk I'd taken from my blackboard in the loft.

"That ought to do it!" I shouted, reeling the tape in.

Scott ran off to the middle of the infield to do his warm-up. I looked down the runway, trying to make sense of my new surroundings. It was beginning to look like a very nice place to pole-vault, except for the cold and windy weather.

"Maggie, you're doing great!" Alex said.

"I haven't even vaulted yet."

"But you're still doing great!"

Alex was obviously overexcited. I smiled. "Okay, now what?" I asked.

"Warm up, same as always!"

I went through my usual warm-up, running and stretching and getting my mind ready to jump. But when I was done, I was colder than when I started.

As I was stretching, Coach Dillinger came up to me and said, "Maggie Steele?"

I nodded. "That's me."

"I've got you listed as a senior. What event are you planning to compete in?"

"Yes, I'm a senior. Um, the pole vault. I'm a pole-vaulter."

He had a troubled expression on his face.

"But you've never been out for track."

"No, sir."

"I see. Well, the pole vault is a pretty difficult event. We could always use another runner."

"No, that's okay, I want to try this," I said. "I brought my own pole."

His eyes brightened. "Where did you get this? I haven't seen one of these in years!"

"My dad bought it a long time ago."

Scott jogged over to join the conversation.

"Have you vaulted with this before?" Coach asked.

"A little."

Coach and Scott exchanged a nervous glance.

"Well, let's see," Coach said. "Scott, we can put the bar as low as it will go."

"But the bar only goes down to seven feet," Scott said.

"Whatever works!" I said, eager to diffuse an awkward situation.

As the coach and Scott put the bar up, I went to my check mark. The icy blast blew in my face. I asked Alex, "What do I do now?"

"Use your six-step mark, hold low. Don't think about the wind."

My eyes watered, my fingers grew numb in my gloves. Everything looked so different than it was in the barn. I was looking at a real pole vault pit with two big pads on either side of the box.

"It's all the same, Maggie," Alex said. "The runway, the box, the crossbar. It's no different than our setup back at the farm."

Coach shouted, "Okay, Maggie, whenever you're ready!" He and Scott were standing close to the box on either side of the runway. They actually looked frightened for me.

"Okay!" I shouted. I took off my gloves and grabbed my cold bamboo pole.

I powered forward, taking aggressive steps into the wind. But just as I planted the pole, a huge gust hit me. As I jumped up in the air, the wind knocked me down. I lost my grip and fell into the box.

Coach and Scott grabbed me by the arms, lifting me back to my feet. "Wow, that was intense!" Scott said.

"Are you okay?" Coach asked.

I nodded, trying not to cry, even though my eyes were watering and my nose was running.

"I want to try again," I said.

"Are you sure?" Coach asked.

I nodded and ran back to my check mark.

"Let's go, Maggie!" Scott shouted. Did I hear sarcasm in his voice? Or was it just the wind?

Alex said, "Okay, okay, move back to your eight-step mark, lean forward. But first wait for the wind to die down a little."

I stood at my mark, waiting, but the wind didn't die down at all. I finally took a deep breath and ran down the runway. I braced myself as I planted the pole and jumped into the wind, expecting another big gust, but it didn't blow. I made it easily! The landing pad was really bouncy, like a giant bed filled with solid foam.

"Nice!" Scott said with a look I'd seen before. He was in love with me again.

"I've seen enough," Coach said, kind of grumpily. "We've never had a girl pole-vaulter before, but you seem determined to do this."

I nodded, smiling. Coach turned his attention to Scott. "I know you can vault. No need risking you getting hurt. Let's put the cover back on the pit."

Coach kept talking as the three of us wrestled with the cover, fastening it back down. "You've *never* had a coach?" he asked me.

"No coach to speak of," I said. I smiled my most convincing smile, but the old coach looked unconvinced.

"Well, that's interesting. Welcome to the team!"

Troy caught up with us as we walked across the football field. I was carrying my pole on my shoulder. "You were awesome!" he said. "Where did you learn to do that?"

"Do what?" I asked. I was messing with him.

"I've never seen anything so beautiful. You looked so graceful. You flew like a bird!"

I felt myself blushing. He had obviously missed my epic crash. "A fat bird in two layers of sweats, maybe." I said. "Besides, I bet you say that to all of your pole-vaulting girlfriends. Here, carry this."

He carried my pole like it was a toothpick. We put it away in the equipment room under the stadium.

"How did your shot-putting go?" I asked.

"I threw forty-eight feet, nine inches."

"Is that good?"

"Well, the next-best guy only threw thirty-eight feet."

"So we both made the team!"

We hugged.

"How did you ever learn to pole-vault?"

"To tell you the truth, it's a big secret."

Troy's handsome face looked puzzled as we walked to our trucks, hand in hand.

"Good night!" I said, kissing him on his frozen lips.

"See you tomorrow!" he said.

I drove home wondering if and when I would be able to share my big secret with him.

CHAPTER 34

Mom and Dad had already eaten, but they were still waiting at the table when I came in.

"Well?" Dad asked.

"I made it, barely!"

I didn't know which I wanted more, to eat a bowl of the vegetable stew I smelled simmering on the stove, or to take a hot shower. I went for the shower. Then I wore my long flannel pajamas and my fuzzy robe and slippers to supper. I told my parents all about the tryout, except I left out the part about me crashing.

My body ached when I got out of bed the next morning. I'd taken only two vaults, but it felt like I'd spent the whole day putting up hay.

I took another hot shower and got dressed for school, packing my sweat clothes and running shoes for practice. I put my stuff in Alex's green GV athletic bag. It carried everything I needed plus a lot of memories.

At school, Scott greeted me like we'd always been friends.

"You did great yesterday, considering that headwind."

"Thanks," I said.

"Usually we get a south wind, but early in the season, you can't predict." He rambled like we were best buds. "It should warm up before the first meet, the Grain Valley Invitational. There'll be a lot of teams coming. You might have some competition."

The bell rang and Scott turned around in his desk. This was going to be different. It was the longest conversation we'd had since forever.

At practice, Coach Dillinger handed out copies of the season schedule to everyone. We were seated on the bleachers in the gym.

"Our first home meet is three weeks away, which might sound like a long time, but it isn't," he said. "Judging from these times from yesterday, it's obvious that some of you haven't run a step since football or volleyball season, except from your TV to the refrigerator." Everybody laughed.

There is a saying about the weather in Kansas: If you don't like it, just wait a day. Sure enough, the weather was different on the day after tryouts. Clouds had rolled in and it was raining. The temperature was warmer than the day before, but it was too wet to go outside.

We did warm-up drills on the basketball court and then jogged in the hallways, which was something I'd never done before, at least without getting yelled at. Troy and the other throwers ran together. Scott jogged beside me, chatting away.

Scott said Coach D, as they called him, didn't know much about coaching pole vault. He had learned by picking up tips from vaulters from other schools, and by listening to what their coaches told them.

"I'm not very good," Scott confessed. "I've only jumped ten-six. But it's fun. And the girls who pole-vault are the best-looking girls on the track." He wiggled his eyebrows at me. I ignored him. "Hey, are you and Troy...?"

"Are we what?"

"Are you going out? I mean, are you serious?"

He was crossing into dangerous territory. "Look, Scott, just because we're teammates doesn't mean you suddenly get to know all about my private life. So cool it, okay? And, yes, Troy and I are going out. I'm not available. End of story. Let's just try to get along." I smiled. "It's a long season."

Scott smiled back. He seemed happy to be let off the hook so easily.

We jogged from the commons area, past the science classrooms and the smell of frogs pickled in formalin. We went up the stairs to the second-floor hallway, past the English classrooms and back down the stairs on the other side, finishing in the commons area again.

We were all laughing and having fun, at least for the first few laps. After five laps my legs felt wobbly, and my lungs started burning in the dry indoor air.

"Keep moving!" Coach Dillinger shouted. "Five more laps! No walking!"

"Five more?" someone moaned, loud enough for Coach Dillinger to hear. "Five more!" he shouted. "Let's go, ladies!" Clearly he meant it as a slur.

It took me about fifteen minutes to run the ten laps. This wasn't fun at all.

"Do not stop!" Coach D bellowed. "Put your hands over your heads! Open up your lungs!"

I locked my fingers together behind my head, flashing back to last summer, when I'd run away from home. I was totally out of breath.

"Good job, Threshers!" Coach shouted. It seemed strange for him to call us ladies one minute and then praise us the next.

It didn't take long before I got my breath back, which was a good thing, because we weren't done running. Coach made us run the ten-lap circuit again and again. After thirty laps, I could barely walk back to the gym. My clothes were drenched with sweat. Coach made us do some stretching exercises on the court. My legs felt rubbery and numb, but it was good to stretch them.

"Good job, Threshers! Drink plenty of water when you get home. Get lots of sleep. See you tomorrow!"

As I dragged myself toward the locker room, as tired as I'd ever been in my life, I felt a big hand on my shoulder. Troy looked down at me, sweaty but smiling. "Hey, you did good!"

I nodded. "That was insane."

"It gets easier, you'll see," he said reassuringly.

"If I survive," I said, only half-joking.

"Hey, if you can make it through the Hallway of Hell, you can make it through anything!"

I smiled. It was a good name for what we'd just been through. "I'm glad I'm a senior. I wouldn't want to go through that again."

I could barely push the clutch pedal down to drive home. I made it into the kitchen and plopped down on my chair. "Coach D is a dungeon master," I moaned. "We ran thirty laps in the hallway."

Dad smiled. "Ah, yes, the Hallway of Hell workout. Your brother always dreaded that one. That's how Coach D finds out who really wants to be on his track team. A lot of people won't show up for practice tomorrow. That's why he waits a few days before handing out the team sweatsuits. The ones who show up are the ones who make the team."

"Good to know, I guess. I hope I can walk by then."

I showed up for the next practice, of course. But I didn't get to pole-vault for the rest of the week. Instead, we either ran or lifted weights or both. Alex had put me through some tough workouts in the loft, but Coach D's regimen was painfully different. I stayed in bed Saturday morning, feeling like I'd played in a football game. But by the end of the second week of practice the soreness was gone, and I was in the best shape of my life.

The following Monday we finally got to go outside. The temperature was in the sixties but the wind was hard from the south, so hard that the crossbar blew off the pegs. Scott wrapped athletic tape around them, making a notch to keep the bar from blowing off.

Coach D posted the roster for the first meet on the bulletin board. The only girl pole-vaulter listed was me.

"Ready or not, here it comes," I said to myself, feeling a jumble of emotions.

CHAPTER 35

On the Friday morning of the Grain Valley Invitational, a south wind blew patches of clouds across the sky. It promised to be a beautiful day, if the rain stayed away.

The principal made the morning announcements. "Everyone is invited to come out to the track meet this afternoon. Field events begin at four, running events at five. Those of you who volunteered to help with the meet, please meet in the gym at 3:30.

"The representative from Washburn University will be on campus today in the commons area."

I wasn't hungry at lunch time, but Troy still made me eat fish sticks, potatoes and gravy, and a couple of cartons of milk, which all tasted really gross. "Does this food taste funny to you?" I asked. "Because it tastes funny to me."

Troy smiled. "Food always tastes different before I play football games. The food is fine."

"But my stomach is churning."

"You'll be fine."

In the locker room after school, I put on my gold track uniform. It was made of a slinky lightweight fabric. I pulled on my team t-shirt. It had *Grain Valley Track and Field* stenciled on the front. On the back it read, *We don't need lame slogans to motivate us!*, which I thought was pretty cool.

I put on my gold sweatpants and hoodie. Coach Dillinger didn't have a lot of money in his budget to pay for fancy uniforms, but I was proud and excited to be wearing this one. I went to the restroom mirror and tied a gold ribbon into my braid.

I looked at my reflection and smiled. "Here we go, Maggie!" I said. "Have fun!"

I shouldered my brother's athletic bag and went out the door toward the stadium. The parking lot was filled with school buses, some from as far away as Eureka.

I walked to the equipment room to get my pole. Athletes were standing in a line under the stadium. Coach Wilson was weighing in shot puts and discuses and javelins. The ones that weighed enough got marked with little green splotches of paint. The ones that were too light were marked red and put into a basket, confiscated until after the meet.

The announcer over the loudspeaker was Miss Jamison, the cheer coach. "First call for the following field events: boys' high jump, boys' shot put, boys' javelin, girls' pole vault, girls' long jump, and girls' discus. Please report to the official at your event immediately!"

I felt a jolt, like I was late for class. I looked for my pole, but it was missing from the shelf. I panicked for a second before I realized that Scott's pole wasn't there either. He must have taken them, I thought. At least I hoped so.

I walked out to the track. The stadium was crowded. I looked for our gold-colored team. We had made camp, so to speak, near the finish line.

There were lots of athletic bags, and every team had a big orange container for water or sports drink. Hurdles had been set up in all the lanes. Nobody was hurdling yet, so I walked across the track and headed for the pole vault pit on the other side of the football field. I could see a line of girls with poles on their shoulders, lined up on the runway. I felt the fish from lunch flopping in my stomach.

"What a beautiful day for a track meet!" Alex said. "Conditions are perfect! You're going to jump amazingly high today, Sis. There's a great tailwind!"

I was about to say something when I saw Scott jogging over to meet me. He was smiling. "I got your pole for you. We're set up over there. You'd better check in with Mr. Bright. He's the official."

I was surprised to see Mark Bright, from the grain elevator. He seemed happy to see me. "Hello, Maggie!" he said. "I saw your name. Are you really vaulting today?"

"I'm really going to try, Mr. Bright," I said. "It's my first real meet."

"Well, I'm afraid the starting height is seven feet, which is as low as the standards will go."

"I know," I said, nodding. "That's fine."

"You're checked in. Go ahead and warm up. We'll get started in about fifteen minutes."

Three or four other girls had come up to check in while Mr. Bright and I had been talking. I heard one of them say that she was going to pass until eight-six. I turned to see a stunning blonde in a dark blue jogging suit. She looked like a fashion model. I'm not kidding. She was the most beautiful high school girl I'd ever seen. I caught Scott staring at her as I jogged over to where our stuff was.

"I'm in love!" he said.

"No, you're in lust. Who is that?"

"That's Amanda McCurdy," he sighed. "Only the hottest girl pole-vaulter in Class 3A, maybe even the entire state. She was second at state last year as a junior, and she's your main competition."

"How high has she vaulted?"

"Eleven feet–something," Scott said. "She's better than I am, but who cares?"

I felt frumpy and plain in my GV warm-ups. "Alex, do you see that girl?" I muttered. "Eleven feet!"

"Oh, that's What's Her Name from Another School. You've jumped against her before, remember?"

I swallowed nervously. "Well, I didn't expect her to be so...so perfect!"

"She's not perfect. But she did have the good fortune of being born to beautiful parents with lots of money. That's them over there, in the matching blue jogging suits. Don't they look grand?"

On the bleachers, just across the track from the pole vault pit, a handsome man was holding a video camera. The woman next to him, also beautiful, held a digital camera with a long telephoto lens.

Miss Jamison came back on the loudspeaker: "Second call for the field events! Please report or be scratched!"

I suddenly realized I had less than five minutes before the event started, and I hadn't even taken a single practice jump.

"You'd better get in line for a run-through," Alex said. "Lucky for you, this is your own runway and your mark is already set."

I took off my hoodie but left my sweat pants and team t-shirt on. I went to the runway and got in line behind a girl from Erie wearing red sweats and carrying a white fiberglass pole.

"Hello? I don't remember seeing you before," said a voice from behind me. It was *her!* "Amanda," she said, extending her hand. Her fingernails were painted the same dark blue as her uniform—not long, but professionally done. She was carrying a flamingo-pink pole. Her smile belonged on the cover of *Vogue*.

"Maggie. Pleased to meet you."

Amanda looked at me for just a moment before glancing at my pole. "What's that?" she asked, snotty like.

"My pole vaulting pole," I said defensively.

"It looks really old. What is it made of?"

"Bamboo."

The girl from Erie was climbing out of the pit. It was my turn.

I heard Alex say, "Well, the introductions went well. Now why don't we focus on what you're here for? This is the pole vault competition, not a fashion show."

I smiled and ran down the runway. My step was perfect. The tail-wind carried me well into the landing pit. I was fired up and ready to go.

Mr. Bright was smiling at me as I got out of the pit. "Where did you get that pole?" he asked. He was looking it over as Amanda ran past. I watched as she jumped into her plant. Her pole bent into a big arc and straightened as she twisted gracefully high over an imaginary bar.

I felt the blood drain out of my face. She was the best vaulter I'd ever seen in real life. In fact, she looked just like the pole-vaulters I'd seen on television.

"What am I doing here?" I whispered to Alex.

The beautiful Amanda stepped gracefully from the landing pad and checked her takeoff mark. Mr. Bright was still talking to me.

"I think I vaulted with this same pole myself, once upon a time."

"You pole-vaulted?" I asked.

"It was my favorite thing in the world," he said, smiling.

"Wow! That's pretty amazing! What are the odds?"

"No kidding! Well, good luck. It's time to get this show on the road."

The girls gathered around to hear Mr. Bright go through the rules, which were just like Alex had explained them, except we weren't on the clock.

"When I call your name, please be ready to go," Mr. Bright said. "First attempt, Steele, Grain Valley."

I hadn't expected to go first, but since it was our home meet, I guess it made sense. I walked up to check my pole against the crossbar.

Two boys from the middle school were helping on each side of the pit. I had them move the standards back so the crossbar was about two feet away from my upright pole.

"Seven feet!" Mr. Bright shouted. "Steele, you're up!"

Alex was waiting for me at the end of the runway. "Okay, Maggie, it's just like we practiced at home. You know what to do. You can make this. Have fun!"

I smiled and nodded, then sprinted down the runway and planted the pole. My shoulder jerked almost out of the socket, but I made it over cleanly. I felt a big sense of relief as I walked off the pad. Mr. Bright was there to hand me my pole. He was smiling.

"Good job!" he said. "Next up, Jones of Chetopa! Jones!"

"You were way over that," Alex said. "But if you're going to run that fast, move your step back a foot."

"Okay," I said, as I sat down.

Scott extended his fist, and I gave it a bump. It felt awkward, but oh well.

"Good start!" he said. "But you might consider wearing just your uniform next time."

I looked at what I was wearing. I'd forgotten to take off my t-shirt and sweat pants.

I didn't get to vault again for nearly twenty-five minutes, which felt really strange. But it took that long for the seven other vaulters who started at seven feet to make it or disqualify themselves. I was really surprised to see three girls go out on the opening height without even coming close. Even I could see that they needed better coaching.

When they finally moved the bar, I made seven-six and eight feet on my first attempts. It felt strange to vault without sweat clothes for the first time.

When the bar got to eight-six, Amanda McCurdy came down from the stands. She'd been sitting with her parents, listening to music on her iPod and texting on her cell phone.

Mr. Bright motioned to the boys, and they moved the crossbar out of the way to allow Amanda to take a warm-up run-through.

"What's that all about?" I asked Scott as we watched her run down the runway.

"It's legal," he said, obviously distracted.

Amanda had taken off her warm-ups for the first time, revealing a spray-tanned body with curves in all the right places. She wore skimpy blue briefs, like a swimsuit bottom. Her uniform top left her belly exposed. She had six-pack abs with not an ounce of fat on her.

"Isn't that illegal?" I asked Scott, referring to the spectacle.

"See why I love this sport?" Scott said, grinning.

I suddenly felt very grateful to Coach D for being so old-school, and that I was wearing an old-fashioned track uniform.

Mr. Bright shouted, "First attempt eight-six, Steele, followed by McCurdy. Steele is up!"

Alex met me at the top of the runway. "Oh, to be young and alive and able to ask hot girls out on dates again."

"Not you too," I hissed, stamping my foot on the runway. "Let's focus here, Alex, and not on her. On me!"

"Okay, that worked. Now that I've helped you build up some emotional steam, let's go!"

As I darted down the runway, a man with a camera around his neck walked in front of me. I had to slam on my brakes.

"Runway! Hey! Watch the runway!" Mr. Bright shouted. The photographer jumped out of my way, or I would have crashed into him. I went back to my check mark and tried to settle down.

"Sorry, Maggie," Alex said. "I saw him coming, but I had no idea he'd walk right in front of you. Take two or three deep breaths and forget about it."

People probably thought I was just nodding to myself. I visualized myself going up and over the bar, and then took off to make it happen.

I cleared the bar—by a lot! But then Amanda McCurdy cleared it by even more.

Scott was drooling. I punched him on the arm. "Hey, teammate! Whose side are you on?" He pulled himself together. "Gosh, Maggie, I mean, you cleared that by a lot!" he said. "And you can go way higher. Don't let Amanda intimidate you. She's been vaulting for years. Goes to the Kansas Jayhawk Pole Vault Camp every summer, has a personal trainer. She'll probably win state, and vault in college. Just forget about her. You're doing great."

I'd never heard Scott put so many well-intentioned thoughts together before. "Thanks," I said. "I really needed to hear that."

Mr. Bright announced, "The bar will be raised to nine-six. There are only two contestants left, Steele and McCurdy. McCurdy's passing nine-six. She's going to run the hurdles and will be back to jump at ten feet, if necessary."

Amanda pulled on her warm-ups and jogged across the field toward the starting line to check in.

"She hurdles, too?" I asked Scott.

Scott nodded, watching her cross the field. "And runs the 100 and the 200 and anchors the 4-by-100 relay. Basically she's in a league of her own."

"Steele's up at nine-six!"

I jumped up, grabbed my pole, shouted for the boys to "put the standards where they were last time," and jogged to my spot on the runway.

I followed Alex's instructions exactly—and made the best vault of my life. I was so happy, I clapped my hands on the way down.

"Nice!" Mr. Bright said, pumping his fist. "You're really good at this!"

The starting gun went off at the far end of the track. Eight girls burst from the starting blocks toward the first hurdle. Amanda was in the middle lane. I watched in amazement as she flew cleanly over one hurdle, and the next, and the next, increasing her lead. She crossed the finish line before the second-place girl had even cleared the last hurdle.

"Impressive!" I said. Scott nodded, but for a different reason. He was clearly under her spell.

"Oh, I forgot to tell you," Scott said. "She's also the defending state champ in the hurdles."

I just rolled my eyes. Clearly, there were some outstanding athletes out here today. And the best girl athlete I'd ever seen was jogging back across the field, looking at me.

"Nice race!" I said.

"Thanks. Did you make nine-six?"

I nodded. Amanda seemed a little surprised, or was she a little put out? I couldn't tell. Mr. Bright came up to us and said, "Maggie, you'll be up first at ten feet, followed by Amanda, when you're ready."

Amanda had just sprinted 100 meters over ten hurdles but wasn't even breathing hard. "I'm ready," she said, acknowledging Scott's ogling with a flirty little wave.

I felt my confidence slipping. Compared to Amanda McCurdy, I was nothing. I walked slowly to the top of the runway. Alex wasn't happy to see me like this.

"You're acting childish!" he scolded. "Amanda McCurdy is a great athlete. So what? That doesn't make you a bad one. You can't compare yourself to her. You have greatness in you, too!" Then he clapped his hands. It sounded like thunder, but nobody heard it but me.

"Let's go, Maggie!" Mr. Bright shouted.

I took my breath and dashed down the runway, faster than ever before. I planted the pole and jumped. Everything felt perfect. I rose up over the bar and pushed the pole away at just the right moment. I leapt from the pad and bounced off the pit, clapping my hands.

"That was excellent!" Mr. Bright said, beaming. "Amazing! Now—McCurdy's up!"

Amanda was standing on the runway with a look of annoyance, or was that worry? But she rode her pole gracefully and made it with a foot to spare.

Instead of feeling jealous, I clapped for her. "Nice!" I said.

"Thanks," she said. "I'm amazed you can jump so high on a fishing pole."

My jaw dropped. Mr. Bright and Scott and I just stood there as Miss Smarty Pants walked over to talk to her parents.

"Pay no attention to her," Mr. Bright said. "That so-called fishing pole of yours has magic in it, I swear! How else can you explain what you're doing here today?"

I thought, *well, it would take a lot of explaining to tell you the truth,* but I just shrugged and smiled a little.

"Move the bar to ten feet six inches!" Mr. Bright shouted to the boys. They had to use helper poles to put the crossbar up that high.

"You can make this," Mr. Bright said to me under his breath. Then he shouted, "Steele up, McCurdy on deck!"

I walked down the runway to my mark. Despite Amanda's put-down, I was elated about making ten feet, my highest vault ever.

Someone up in the stands shouted, "Go, Maggie!" I looked over and saw Mom and Dad and Grandma. I waved at everybody, feeling excited and encouraged.

It took a long time to get up there, it was so high. I don't really remember pushing the pole or landing on the pad, and it took even longer to get down. But I do remember bouncing, and then Mr. Bright and Scott hugging me and pounding me on the back.

On the loudspeaker, Miss Jamison said, "That's Maggie Steele from Grain Valley, over the bar at ten feet six inches!"

In the stands, Mom and Dad were hugging each other. Grandma was hopping up and down, giving me two thumbs up. People were going a little nuts about this.

Mr. Bright pulled himself together, remembering that he was the official. "Okay now, everybody clear out, we still have another vaulter left in the competition! McCurdy's up!"

Amanda was without a doubt not happy with the celebration she'd just witnessed. She stood at her check mark with a scowl on her face, but her eyes flashed with determination. She powered down the runway and cleared the bar by at least six inches.

"Wow! Great jump!" I shouted. But none of the people who had been cheering for me joined in the celebration.

"The bar will be going to eleven feet!" Mr. Bright said, sounding amazed. "Maggie Steele is up, followed by McCurdy!"

For some reason, I couldn't catch my breath. I tried to sprint down the runway, but I felt too tired. I planted the pole well and rode high in the air, but knocked the bar down on my first attempt.

I watched Amanda dash down the runway. Her steps were perfect. Her pink pole bent nearly in half as she hung beneath it. She rode it up and over the bar, curving her perfect body over it, quite beautifully.

"That's Amanda McCurdy from St. Bishop Academy over the bar at eleven feet, which is a new meet record, breaking the record she set last year at ten feet six inches!" Miss Jamison said. "Grain Valley's Steele has two attempts remaining."

But I missed my last two tries. I was too pooped to vault any higher, but I had done pretty well, right? Mr. Bright extended his scarred hand and said, "Your brother would have been happy to see this today."

"Thanks, Mr. Bright," I said. "Thanks for everything."

He smiled and walked away, carrying his clipboard to the press box, wiping his eyes.

CHAPTER 36

The following Monday the principal made these announcements: "Congratulations to the Threshers, who did so well at the Grain Valley Invitational on Friday. In the boys' shot put, Troy Timmerman placed first with a throw of fifty feet, eight inches! In the girls' pole vault, Maggie Steele placed second in her first track meet, with a vault of ten feet, six inches, establishing the school record! Thanks to the volunteers who helped at the meet....The representative from Tabor College will be on campus today....And, seniors, your graduation ceremony will be held on Sunday afternoon, May 27th. That's five weeks away!"

A cheer went up in the calculus class, followed by an outburst of chatter back and forth. Scott turned around and started babbling, like we were best friends.

"Thank God it's almost over," he said. "I can't wait to get out of this school, out of this town, out of this state!"

"You're going away?"

"Soon as I take off my cap and gown, I'm out of here. I'm going back to Boise, where we came from."

"You're from Idaho? Really? I didn't—"

"I'm going to play quarterback at Boise State as a walk-on," Scott continued. "I've always wanted to play on that blue field, ever since I was a little kid; we had season tickets when I was growing up, before we moved here."

"Good luck with that," I said, trying to sound optimistic. I was thinking about his fumbles and interceptions and what the coaches would think when he got off the bus. I was surprised by his enthusiasm for leaving. We'd been enemies for so long, but now we were sort of friends. Soon, Scott would be gone, along with the rest of my class.

I realized that these people I'd gone to school with wouldn't be the ones I grew older with. I looked at Scott differently at that moment. He didn't have much of a chance of playing football for Boise State or any other college team. But at least he was going away someplace, and at least he had a dream, which was more than I could say for myself.

In the hallway after class, people said, "Way to go, Maggie!" and "I saw you pole-vaulting!" and "You're amazing!" and "I could never do that!" I felt kind of sort of famous, in a small-school kind of way.

I hadn't spent a lot of time worrying about what I was going to do after graduation. I focused on pole vaulting and homework, pretending that I really didn't have to decide how I was going to spend the rest of my life. After scoring a respectable 29 on the ACT, I'd been getting envelopes from colleges and universities all over the country, many addressed to Margaret Ann Steele. The envelopes were filled with letters and brochures with glossy pictures of leafy campuses and happy students, with slogans like: *You belong here!* and *Start here, go anywhere!*

I got so many of them that Mom put a shoebox in the kitchen to put them in, to keep them from piling up. Then she got a bigger box because the shoebox was filled to overflowing. Finally she found a plastic tub for them. I must have gotten a hundred. At first I read them. I was looking for one of them to grab me and to say "Here it is! This is the place!" but none of them did.

Now, less than a month before I would graduate, most of the letters hadn't even been opened. I realized that every senior in the entire nation who'd scored well on the ACT had boxes filled with marketing materials, like I did. I'd gone from feeling flattered and wanted to feeling deluged by junk mail.

Left unsaid at the dinner table at our house was how my decision would affect the future of the Steele family farm. My parents had been having a lot of closed-door discussions lately, talking late into the night.

Scott's decision to go back to Idaho reminded me what I'd been trying to forget. My stomach churned as I went up to the loft after supper to talk to Alex. When I got there, I wasn't sure where to begin.

"What's wrong?" Alex asked.

"You know, I'm really mad at you."

"For what?"

"For leaving me, with this."

"With what?"

"This farm! With you gone, it's up to me now, to keep it going."

"Are you sure about that? Have you talked to Dad and Mom?"

"I don't have to talk to them. I don't want to talk to them. I can see it on their faces. They're expecting me to take your place, and I don't want to go through what happened last summer—harvesting and baling and planting and all the rest of it—for the rest of my life."

There was a long silence. Finally Alex said, "Well, there may be another option."

"Like what?"

"Like maybe you can vault your way out of here."

I laughed. "You know, you're funnier now that you're dead."

"Seriously, they give college scholarships for girls' pole vaulting nowadays, if you're good enough."

I sighed. "I don't know if I'm good enough for college pole vaulting. Heck, I'm still trying to figure out how I've become a *high school* pole-vaulter. How did I ever get to go this high so fast? I mean, think about it. Who would've believed it? How is any of this even possible?"

"It's possible because it isn't impossible. For starters, I know everything there is to know, which makes my coaching exactly what you need to hear. And second, you're always willing to do exactly what I'm telling you. And you try your best, every time."

I nodded in agreement. He went on. "You've always had the speed, strength, and daring to be a great vaulter; I'm just giving you the know-how. Don't forget that you've always been a special athlete, even though you didn't do sports. You won the Presidential Physical Fitness Award every year from the first grade on, didn't you? And you never lost a race on field day."

I thought about the red, white, and blue certificates lining the wall in my bedroom, next to all the ribbons from the sheep shows.

"And Maggie?"

"What?"

"You're also the bravest girl I've ever known."

"I don't feel so brave right now, about the future."

"How about we take on the future together, one day, one vault at a time?"

"Only if you promise not to leave me."

"I'll always be with you, Maggie."

An ominous thunderstorm rolled in at practice on Monday. It brought thunder and lightning and a dark wall of rain that we could see barreling down on us. When a big bolt of lightning hit nearby, Coach Dillinger blew his whistle and waved everyone inside.

"Cover the pit! Grab your poles and the crossbar and get to the building!"

Scott and I pulled the cover over the pit, but it ballooned like a parachute, and it took forever to get it hooked down. We made a mad dash for the school, but before we got there the storm hit, and we were completely drenched by giant drops of cold rain. Coach held the door open for us as lightning flashed overhead.

"Here, give me those poles!" he said. "You guys go ahead and get dried off. I'll see you tomorrow." Instead of taking our stuff back out in the rain to the equipment room under the stadium, he opened the door in the hallway and put everything in the boiler room.

The next day before practice, Coach D opened the boiler room door. A blast of hot air poured out on us.

"Holy crap! Look at my pole!"

"What's wrong?" Coach D asked.

I turned the pole in his direction. The crack went all the way from one end of the pole to the other. I could see its hollow insides.

Coach took a roll of white athletic tape out of the pouch he wore around his waist and started wrapping it around the pole. He pulled tightly on the tape, trying to pull the cracked opening closed as he wound. But after using an entire roll of tape, he wasn't even halfway up the pole.

"Come on," he said, walking down the hallway back to the locker room.

I felt sick to my stomach but didn't say anything. Coach acted like he knew what he was doing. He spent almost fifteen minutes wrapping my pole in white tape.

"Well, it only took three rolls, but that should do it. Go out and give it a try."

Coach never said he was sorry, exactly, but I could tell he felt really bad. When I got out to the track, Scott was busy bailing rainwater out of the box. He pointed at my pole and shook his head.

"Trying to make it look like fiberglass, right? You can tell that's just tape on there you know," Scott said.

"Shut up." I was in no mood for jokes.

"What happened?" he asked, backing up.

I took my bandaged pole to my mark on the runway and turned my back to wipe my eyes. I wasn't about to let Scott see me cry.

"Uh-oh!" Alex said. "Looks like you've got a fatally fractured bamboo pole there, Maggie. But let's see. Give it a try."

The bar was only seven feet. I ran down the runway and planted the pole. It sagged weirdly, collapsing under my weight. I barely had enough momentum to make it to the landing pad. Of course, I missed badly.

"Holy cow! Are you all right?" Scott shouted. "Your pole's broken! It bent crooked!"

I climbed out of the pit. My temper was boiling, and I felt angry and scared. Coach D was jogging in my direction.

I grabbed the pole and flung it on the ground. I yelled at him to keep from bawling. "It doesn't work! It's broken! I don't have another pole! I'm going home!"

I left the pole lying where I'd thrown it, bent and beyond repair.

"We can find you another one," Coach said as I stomped past.

I choked on my words. "That bamboo pole was an antique. They don't make them anymore. You can't find them anymore. How am I going to vault without a pole?"

I went into the locker room, but instead of changing my clothes, I just grabbed everything, shoved it into my bag, and ran to the parking lot. Then I drove home, sadder than I'd been since you-know-when.

I went up to the loft and sat down on a bale of straw, holding my head in my hands. One of the cats curled up in my lap, purring and kneading my leg.

"It's all over," I sobbed. "Coach D broke my pole! What am I going to do now?"

Alex tried to console me. "I'm so sorry, Maggie. I didn't see this coming—not that I could have prevented it from happening. But it was an accident. Coach Dillinger didn't mean to break your pole. He obviously feels terrible about it. I'm sure he'll come up with some way to get you another one."

"What's he going to do, fly to Asia to cut me a new piece of bamboo? That pole was one of a kind. I should've never let him put it in the boiler room." I was still mad, but at least I wasn't crying anymore.

"You couldn't have known. Sometimes things just happen. Some people up here believe that everything happens for a reason, for the greater good."

"What possible good could come from this?"

Alex didn't respond, allowing me to think my own thoughts. I rejected the idea that learning to pole-vault had been a big waste of time. I mean, if I hadn't learned to pole-vault, I wouldn't have my brother back, right?

But now, with my pole broken...

"Does this mean you won't be around anymore?" I asked. "I don't want to you to leave. I need you. For everything."

I buried my head and cried some more.

"It may seem like everything is broken, but something big is about to happen," Alex said. "Let's see what happens in the next few days."

"Okay," I sniffled. "But I need to know one thing. Will you still be here, even if we aren't pole-vaulting?"

"I'm always with you, Sis. No matter what."

I left the loft feeling better. I was willing to leave room for the remote possibility that everything would work out. And I slept okay, considering my world had cracked and broken.

CHAPTER 37

Coach Dillinger called me aside before practice. He was frowning. He said he was sorry but he couldn't buy me a new pole because his track budget had been spent.

"But I've talked to the activities director," he said. "He said the principal would have to get special permission from the school board to make an emergency request. The good news is that the board meets tonight, so it could all be resolved quickly.

"We all want you to keep vaulting," Coach D continued. "We're proud of you. Until we can get you another pole, please keep working out with the team. You can lift weights, run sprints, help Scott, that sort of thing."

"Okay," I said. I was not optimistic, to say the least.

That night, Dad and I took his old truck to the board office to sit in on the big meeting. I noticed there was a new crack in the windshield. When I looked at Dad's hands on the steering wheel, I saw wrinkles on them I hadn't seen before. My dad had aged five years in the last one.

"Let's see how this goes," he said as we parked and went in.

The board met in a conference room around a big table. There were chairs for visitors, so we sat. A man dressed in a suit was also seated. I hadn't thought about dressing up for the meeting. I had on my Grain Valley track hoodie, blue jeans, and running shoes, and wore a GV cap over my braided hair. Dad took off his feed cap, so I took my hat off too.

I recognized most of the board members. Mr. Bright was one of them. He smiled and waved. Rev. Stark was also on the board. Everyone seemed to be in a good mood as they shuffled papers that were being passed around. When the clock on the wall read seven, Mr. Ballinger, the board president, tapped a wooden gavel on the table to bring the meeting to order.

"The regular monthly meeting of the Grain Valley School Board is now in session," he said. "The clerk has handed out the agenda for tonight's meeting. Are there any corrections or additions to the minutes?"

The school principal, the activities director, and Coach Dillinger came through the door at that moment and sat in the visitors' chairs beside us, quietly, out of respect for the proceedings already in progress.

The principal raised his hand. "Mr. President, we have one matter to be discussed under new business at the appropriate time."

The minutes were approved as read, whatever that means. The man in the suit was an insurance agent. He told the board that health insurance was going up twenty-five percent, which put all of the board members in a bad mood. It was 8:15 before they were ready to discuss new business.

"You said you have something for us, Mr. Taylor?" the president asked.

"Yes, I do. Thank you. I have an emergency request from the track coach and activities director for a special purchase, to buy a girls' pole vault pole for Maggie Steele."

I wasn't expecting the principal to mention me by name. Everyone looked at me and I blushed. I lifted my hand in a sort of half wave and smiled a little.

"Maggie's out for track this spring," Mr. Taylor explained, "and if you were there at the meet Friday night, you saw her jump ten feet six inches, which is as good as anybody else at school right now."

Rev. Stark shifted uneasily in his seat. Mr. Bright smiled.

"Miss Steele had been using her own vaulting pole, an old-time bamboo pole that her father purchased at the school auction years ago. But that pole was broken beyond repair when Coach Dillinger here put it in the boiler room.

"I'm bringing this to the board's attention tonight because we have never had a girl pole-vaulter and have no pole for her to use. The boys' poles are simply too big. Normally I would have simply approved the purchase of a new pole for Maggie, but our track budget is spent for this year. With the spending freeze in effect, I'm coming to you to make an emergency request."

"How much are we talking about?"

"With shipping, four hundred and eight dollars."

Someone whistled. The president pounded his gavel. "We have an emergency request from the high school principal in the amount of four hundred eight dollars for a girls' pole vaulting pole. Is there any discussion?"

Three or four board members raised their hands.

"Reverend Stark?"

The reverend shuffled papers with his stubby fingers. The sight of his gold pinky ring brought back bad memories.

"I watched Maggie vault on Friday," he said, smiling in my direction. "You did very well, especially considering this is your first year out for track, and apparently you've had no real coaching. Having said this, I'm just not convinced that pole vaulting is an appropriate activity for females."

The board members started talking amongst themselves. The gavel pounded.

The reverend continued, "My son says you've taken a couple of bad spills. It just seems awfully dangerous to me. And in light of what we've heard tonight about our unexpected expenses, I would not be in favor of us making this purchase."

I felt Dad stiffen in his chair. He opened his mouth to say something, then closed it, shaking his head.

"Any other discussion?" the president asked. "Mr. Bright?"

"I ran the pole vault on Friday. I want to say, for the record, that I've never been more impressed by a Grain Valley athlete. Maggie was using the same bamboo pole I vaulted with at the old K–8 school back in the sixties. Mr. Steele here bought the pole and the old standards and everything at the consolidation auction."

Dad nodded. "I got everything for eighty-five dollars, if I remember right."

"Well, the price of equipment has gotten a whole lot more expensive since then, hasn't it?" Rev. Stark asked. Everybody laughed, but not because it was funny.

"I think girls have proven that they can pole-vault, even though we haven't had any at our school until Maggie started," Mr. Bright said. "There were nine girls vaulting on Friday. It's getting more and more popular. By law, I think we need to provide equal opportunity for them." He looked directly at Rev. Stark. "The boy pole-vaulters have several school-bought poles. The reverend's son uses one of them. He made ten feet at our meet, am I correct?"

Mr. Bright paused and let everyone catch up to the fact that I had vaulted higher than Scott. The reverend's face was bright red.

"Scott has access to the poles we purchased, Reverend," Mr. Bright said. "We haven't asked you to buy one for him. Fact is, pole vaulting is expensive. There are thousands of dollars' worth of equipment wrapped up in the event." He looked at Coach Dillinger. "How much did that new landing mat cost?"

"About fourteen thousand dollars," Coach D said.

The discussion went on for half an hour. The board members seemed sympathetic, but they kept coming back to the fact that the track money had already been spent.

When the president put the matter to a vote, Mr. Bright and the only woman board member voted for me, but my new pole was defeated, four to two.

The meeting adjourned and Dad left quickly, which was his way. I followed him to the truck, wondering how Alex could have been so wrong about the way things were turning out.

CHAPTER 38

Dad never said anything about buying me a new pole, so I didn't ask. He spent a lot of time alone in the shop working on the combine after that. After all, the next wheat harvest was less than two months away. As life on the farm continued, my life had fallen apart.

I stayed away from track practice. After all, my season was over, so what was the point? I also avoided going up to the loft, because I was afraid that when I went up there, Alex would be gone.

But Big Troy was a good listener. He seemed to know how important pole vaulting had been to me, though he didn't know why. I felt like keeping the secret from him made everything worse. But no way could I tell him about Alex. He would think I was seriously crazy, and I needed his friendship.

On Friday, Troy and the rest of the track team were out of town, at the Chanute Invitational. I was alone and feeling sorry for myself, so I went next door to Grandma's after supper.

"Come in! Come in!" she said, opening the screen door. I reached for a hug, and she held me for a long time.

The late evening sun put a golden glow on everything in the living room. I sat down on the couch.

"What's on your mind, dear?"

I took a deep breath and let out a heavy sigh. "I've got less than a month until graduation, and I have no idea what I'm going to do with my life."

Grandma's hazel eyes sparkled behind her thick glasses. A smile lit up her entire face. "I've been holding spiritual space for you," she said. Her voice sounded like a melody. "You have everything you need in order to do that which is meant for you to do."

I didn't understand what she meant, but I went home from Grandma's feeling better about my uncertain future.

That night I dreamed that Dad and Mom and Alex and me and Grandma and Grandpa were in our wheat field, harvesting, using the old-fashioned threshing equipment from the barn. I saw us walking home together behind a grain-filled wagon. Everything was pulled by horses. We were dressed in the clothes they wore a hundred years ago. The men wore broad-brimmed hats and suspenders over white shirts. All the women, including me, wore long dresses and white sunbonnets. As evening fell across the harvested field, we saw a full moon rising.

"That's Maggie's moon," Alex said.

And Grandma said, "Yes, it is. That's Maggie's moon."

When I woke up from my dream, it was Saturday. I found Mom and Dad sitting at the kitchen table. I bent over and kissed Dad on his salt-and-pepper head, and I kissed Mom on the cheek. I poured myself a cup of coffee, adding lots of sugar, just the way I like it. Then I said, "You know, I had the most amazing dream last night. Let me tell you about it..."

I talked nonstop for about ten minutes about all of us working in the harvest field, and about Maggie's moon. Mom and Dad just sat there, not saying anything.

"What do you think it means?"

Mom and Dad exchanged glances, still not talking.

"What's the matter?" I asked.

Mom seemed to choose her words carefully. "Your Dad and I have been up for about an hour now, trying to make sense of it ourselves."

"Make sense of what?"

"Maggie, your mom and I dreamed that very same dream," Dad said.

I felt the hair rise up on the back of my neck.

There was a gentle knock on the back door. Dad got up to open it.

"Good morning! Do I smell coffee?" said Grandma, coming in. "I just had to come over to see you because I had the most wonderful dream!"

At that moment, the doorbell rang. We just sat there looking at each other. The bell rang a second time. Dad pushed his chair back and headed toward the living room. Mom and Grandma and I followed him.

Mr. Bright was standing on the porch. "Hello, Maggie!" he said. "Could you come outside? I've got something for you."

We walked out onto the porch into the bright morning sunlight. Mr. Bright's truck was parked in the driveway. A white long cardboard tube was tied up against the passenger side. The words "GILL Athletics" were printed on it in red ink, spinning around like a candy cane.

"Sorry this took so long to get here," he said, using his pocketknife to cut the twine that held the tube on. He opened the wrapper at end of the tube and shook it. A long florescent-green pole slid out and he handed it to me.

"What's that?" Grandma asked.

"It's a fiberglass pole!" I said. It felt remarkably light. A decal wrapped around the pole said *Skypole* in light purple lettering, along with a yellow lightning bolt, like the pole contained electricity or something.

"I got it from Bell Athletics," Mr. Bright said. "That's Earl Bell's outfit. I wasn't sure what size you needed so I called and talked to him personally on the phone."

"Who?" I said.

Mr. Bright laughed. "Earl Bell! The former world record-holder and three-time Olympic pole-vaulter. He coaches the best vaulters in the country at his camp down in Jonesboro, Arkansas. I told him all about you."

I couldn't believe what I was hearing, or what I was holding in my hands. "You did?"

"That's the pole he recommended for you. Oh, and another thing. He said something kind of peculiar. He said, 'You be sure to tell Maggie that she'll jump clear over the moon on this one!'"

Mom and Dad and Grandma and me all looked at each other, thunderstruck. But Mr. Bright didn't notice. "I almost forgot!" he said, and opened the passenger door of his truck. He handed me a box made of recycled cardboard with blue printing on it. "When I was online, I also ordered you a pair of spikes. They looked perfect for pole-vaulters."

The label read "Brooks, PR MD size 9."

"How'd you know my size?" I asked.

"I asked Troy Timmerman to do some spying. He got the size of your running flats, so I got the same size, same brand."

I opened the box and moved the tissue paper. "They're green, awesome! They match my pole!" I gave Mr. Bright a hug.

"You'll need to be sprinting full speed to get up on that pole," he said.

My parents and Grandma had come off the porch. They stood beside me, not believing what they saw. "It sure is a pretty thing," Grandma said, touching the pole with her wrinkled hands. "This is a real fine thing you've done here, mister, a mighty fine thing."

Mr. Bright tipped his hat.

"What do we owe you?" Dad asked, shaking Mr. Bright's hand. Scar tissue crisscrossed his knuckles. "Well, let me think." Mr. Bright smiled. "I get off at noon today, and I'd sure like to see Maggie try her new pole. Can we meet at the stadium for a tryout?"

I nodded, smiling.

As he drove away, I stood there dumbfounded.

"Well isn't that something!" Grandma said.

CHAPTER 39

There were several cars and trucks parked in front of the stadium when we drove up shortly after noon. Dad parked our van next to Mr. Bright's pickup. My new pole was strapped to the luggage rack. Troy got out of his truck and came over with the biggest smile on his face.

"Did you have anything to do with all these people showing up?" I asked, hugging him with all my might.

He laughed. "Believe it or not, I didn't say anything to anybody."

Coach Dillinger got out of his car and waved. As he went to unlock the gate, Troy helped Dad take my new pole off the van. Mom and Grandma took stuff out of the back, a couple of lawn chairs and a cooler with snacks and drinks in it.

"Looks like we're having a pole vault picnic!" Grandma said.

Another car door slammed. I was surprised to see Scott Stark.

"Hey, Maggie! Welcome back. I came to help you get the cover off the pit," he said with a laugh. I smiled, forgetting any hard feelings. After all, we were teammates.

A woman got out of her car with a girl of about ten. She introduced herself as Mrs. Hendrickson, and her daughter as Holly. I remembered her from the school board meeting. Holly Hendrickson was cute, with a splash of freckles on her nose. She reminded me of me at that age.

I was shaking her little hand when someone grabbed me from behind around the leg of my sweatpants.

"Maggie!" shouted Zackary.

"Hey, Zack-a-roo!" I held him up and hugged him.

"Dad said you get to pole-vault again, and I came to watch!"

Coach Wilson walked over, smiling. "Thanks to Mr. Bright, Grain Valley's best pole-vaulter is back in action!" he said.

We walked across the football field to the pole vault pit. Zack carried my warm-up bag, shouldering the burden like a little man. By the time we got there, Scott and Coach Dillinger had the cover off the pit and the standards all set up. It was a beautiful day for vaulting.

"I need to warm up," I said, jogging away from the group.

"Hey, Alex? Are you here?" I whispered.

"Afternoon, Maggie!" Alex shouted.

My heart leapt into my throat.

"How about that Mr. Bright? Some kind of hero, isn't he?"

It was great to hear his voice again. "You're going to jump really high on that pole," Alex went on. "Picked out for you special by Earl Bell himself. How cool is that? He's the best pole vault coach in the nation, maybe the world!"

"Thanks for being here," I said.

"I wouldn't have missed it. Warm up really good. You need to be sprinting full speed. And how about those new spikes! Those are the coolest shoes I've ever seen!"

I warmed up like I was getting ready for a big meet. My heart raced. I was as excited and ready as I'd ever been.

My new fiberglass pole was about two feet longer than my bamboo pole had been, but it weighed about the same. I really didn't have a clue how to use it. When it came time for my first vault, I felt like I was starting all over again. "See that lightning bolt there on the Skypole logo?" Alex said. "That tells you everything you need to know."

"How's that?"

"The big difference between this pole and your bamboo pole is that this pole gives back all the energy, all the power that you put into it, at just the right time."

I felt a jolt of excitement. I just had to try it.

I ran down and planted my new pole just like always. It bent a lot, and then straightened with a lot of force, throwing me into the air, totally sideways! I landed on my feet on the right front pad. My heart was racing. It felt like I'd been shot out of a cannon.

"Wow! That was intense!" Scott said, blinking. Coach Dillinger and Mr. Bright stood there open-mouthed.

"Don't worry," I said. "We're going to get this figured out."

I went back to my starting point. "It's alive," I said in my best Frankenstein voice.

"Indeed it is!" Alex said. "It's going to bend a lot more than your bamboo pole, but you have to trust it. It's the perfect pole for you. It's not going to break."

"But do I need to do anything different?" I asked.

"Nope, you are fundamentally sound, and ready to take full advantage of the added boost you can get from fiberglass. Now you can hold higher, and get back all the energy you put in when you plant the pole. Just hold on tight and enjoy the ride!"

I ran down the runway and jammed the pole into the box. The pole bent to my left, but I focused on staying balanced, just like I'd learned from the start. My new pole bent a lot more, and then it sprang back with great force, shooting me in the air.

"Awesome!" Zack shouted. "You flew really high!"

"Do you want to try it with a crossbar?" Mr. Bright asked.

"What do you think?" I said. I was asking Alex, but nobody knew that.

"Put it on eleven feet and see what happens," Alex said.

"Eleven feet?" I said.

"Eleven feet it is!" Mr. Bright said. Everybody cheered.

I went to the top of the runway and did exactly what Alex said, all over again. The pole unbent and I launched like a rocket. I cleared the bar by a mile and kept going up and up, before falling way down to the landing pad.

I felt like I'd just got back from outer space. Troy helped me out of the pit and gave me a hug as everyone crowded around.

"Holy cow!" Mr. Bright said. "That Earl sure knows how to pick a pole!"

I nodded. It was amazing. I was pole-vaulting again!

CHAPTER 40

The Walnut Valley League track meet was held at our track on the following Friday, but instead of balmy temperatures and a perfect tailwind from the south, like we had enjoyed on Saturday, it felt like the weatherman had flipped the calendar back a month or two.

Mom and Dad sat in the stands, bundled up in blankets like at a football game. It was too cold for Grandma, so she stayed home. With the north wind blowing in my face, it took all my effort just to make eleven feet again. But I managed to snake over it, win the gold medal, and improve on my own school record, so that was cool. Amanda McCurdy wasn't there because St. Bishop belonged to a different league. Another vaulter told me that Amanda had already vaulted twelve feet this season, which seemed really impressive to me.

The award stand was set up on the football field near the place where I'd been crowned homecoming queen. As I stood on top of the platform to accept my gold medal, Miss Jamison made a big deal out of the ceremony over the loudspeaker. "And the first-place gold medal winner, with a new school record and new league meet record vault of eleven feet, Maggie Steele of Grain Valley!"

A lot of wonderful things had happened so far this year, but I had a feeling that the best was yet to come. I couldn't wait to see how high I could go on a good day.

Monday morning, it was time for the principal's usual announcements: "Congratulations to our league champions! Troy Timmerman won the gold medal in the shot put Friday with a heave of fifty-two feet, and Maggie Steele won the pole vault with a vault of eleven feet! That's another school record!

"The track teams will compete at regionals at Erie on Friday. The top four finishers in each event qualify for the state championships in Wichita.

"There are thirteen days until graduation. Seniors, if you want to receive your diploma, you must return your overdue library books and pay your fines. See Mrs. Lane before the last day of school, which for all you lucky seniors is this Friday!"

I must confess that, being so focused on pole vaulting, my final exams had caught up with me. I had to spend the entire weekend cramming for finals in calculus, history, and science. I also had to finish a ten-page paper for English. It was like somebody had decided that if the seniors at Grain Valley were getting out a week early, we'd have to do two weeks' worth of school work in our last week of high school to make up for it.

There were several seniors in my calculus class who could barely keep their eyes open. They'd been up all night studying. I'd turned out my light at two a.m., so I'd gotten a little sleep. But still, a calculus final at eight in the morning on the last Monday of your senior year was cruel and unusual punishment. Although it had always been that way at Grain Valley, so I guess it wasn't unusual, just cruel. I turned in my test hoping for an A, but a B would be okay. At that point I would even have taken a C.

After two hours of number-crunching, my brain was fried. I leaned up against the lockers, my head spinning. I opened my eyes to see Betsy Miller standing in front of me. She looked sad. There were dark circles under her eyes.

"I'm so glad that's over," I sighed. "That was a nightmare."

Betsy nodded. I could tell she had something other than calculus on her mind.

A lot of seniors were feeling nostalgic about graduating, because of everything and everyone we'd be leaving behind. Betsy and I had drifted apart, so I thought maybe she was going to say something about that, but what she told me really blew my mind.

"We're moving," she said, tears welling in her eyes.

I was glad I was already leaning against the lockers.

"The realtor put a sign up yesterday afternoon, so it's official. We're moving to Kansas City. The moving van is coming Wednesday after graduation."

"I'm so sorry," I said.

"It's for the best, really," Betsy said. "My parents and I, we need a new start. But I'll miss you."

We hugged each other tight, and then we cried and cried.

The bell rang. We were late for our history final!

Someone must've told the teacher about our "senior moment," because he didn't say anything to us when we came in late. My head was pounding. I sat for five minutes before I took out my pen.

CHAPTER 41

I announced the big news to my parents at supper.

"The Millers are moving!"

Dad nodded. "I knew that," he said, chewing.

"You knew? Why didn't you say anything?"

"Didn't want to upset you. It wasn't a for-sure thing, and you had other things to worry about."

Too late. I was upset. "I just found out, Betsy told me. It sucks."

Mom frowned at my choice of words, but nobody said anything else.

I clanked my plate with the spoon, shaking mashed potatoes onto my plate. I was tired and hungry and my head still hurt. And now I was finding out that my parents had been keeping secrets. I clanked my plate again with the green bean spoon.

Dad got up and went out to the shed. Mom and I went through the motions of clearing the table and doing the dishes. Whatever we were thinking we kept in our own heads.

Finally I said, "I've got a science final tomorrow. I'm going to study."

I took my bookbag into my room and closed the door. A breeze was blowing in the open window, and it was beautiful outside, but it didn't matter. I lay on my bed, just breathing.

I woke up to the alarm. I'd slept all night with my school clothes on. Mom had gone to town and Dad was in the shed. I ate cold cereal for breakfast and went to school.

The science final was ridiculously easy, but I was still upset, like I'd been knocked out of the saddle.

"Earth to Maggie!" Troy said.

We were eating lunch. I was poor company. "Sorry, I'm out to lunch today," I said, a pathetic little joke.

He looked at me with sympathy. He knew all about my episode with Betsy in the hallway.

"You had a triggering event," he said.

"A what?"

"Betsy's announcement forced you to think about things you haven't been thinking about. Your emotions went off, like a trigger on a gun."

"It felt more like a bomb, but thank you for the diagnosis, Dr. Timmerman."

He held my hands. His were warm and strong.

"I thought I was getting better," I said. He nodded. Students walked past, chatting and carrying their cafeteria trays.

"It's just that I still don't know what I'm going to do, and it's time to know, you know?"

He smiled. "Just in time," he said.

"What?"

"Just in time. It's a thing I read about. It's how companies build cars. They don't have all of the parts at the factory all at once. They fix it so the parts show up exactly when they're needed, just in time."

I put down my fork. "Okay, but what does that have to do with me?"

"I'm talking about you, Maggie. You and your life, and the decisions you're trying to make about your future."

"But I'm not a Toyota."

Troy laughed. "No, you're more like a BMW, I think."

"The point?" I asked, smiling at the compliment.

"The point is, you're still on the assembly line, and the parts are in still in shipment. That is, it's all coming together for you, like clockwork, but you don't see it yet."

"Isn't that a mixed metaphor or something?" I was pulling his chain.

"Okay, listen, smarty. Here it is: I believe in you. You have a bright future. Everything will come together. Just don't stop doing what you've been doing to get there."

"To get where?"

"That's the point! I'm going to K State. But remember, I had no idea where I was going until the offer came, just in time." He looked so handsome, so serious.

"Okay then, Doctor. I'll accept your diagnosis and your prescription. But only if you give it to me with a little sugar." I leaned over and kissed him on the lips, right there in the cafeteria.

Then I said, "Thanks, Dr. Timmerman, I think I'm cured!"

CHAPTER 42

Our team bus rolled toward Erie shortly after noon on Friday. Troy and I sat together, holding hands, watching the Kansas countryside. The wheat was almost ready to harvest.

An hour later we saw a sign that read, "Welcome to Erie, Home of the Red Devils."

"The whole Erie Devils thing seems creepy to me," I said.

"Me toooo," Troy said in a spooky voice.

"They have the devil himself as their mascot!" I fake-shivered. "Children here grow up cheering for devils and wanting to be devils. Kind of *eerie*, don't you think?"

"Yeeesss, I dooo," Troy said, playing along.

We rolled down Main Street past the combined Methodist/Presbyterian church. I wondered how the church folk felt about cheering for Satan. I wondered what Scott's dad would have said if his son had been quarterbacking the Devils' football team. Thinking about Rev. Stark made me think about his comments against girl pole-vaulters and leading the vote against me. I started to get upset about it all over again, but then remembered that, while he might have been able to keep the district from buying me a new pole, he hadn't stopped me from pole-vaulting.

The new track at Erie was located in what must've been some farmer's wheat field, about a quarter mile north of town. As we pulled up to the stadium, several other buses were already parked on the blacktop. I felt excited about being part of something as cool as a regional track meet. There would be sixteen teams here. The first four finishers in each event qualified for the state meet next Friday and Saturday in Wichita. As we got off the bus, I kissed Troy and wished him good luck in the shot put. He hugged me and said, "Have fun!"

Scott and I pulled our poles out of the back emergency door of the bus. The alarm went off, as usual, adding drama to the moment.

"We're in Eeerieee!" I said, in a spooky voice. "It's sooo alarming!"

Scott laughed at my corny joke. He was nervous, too. He'd been to regionals for three years but had never finished in the top four, and this was his last chance. With me in front and Scott behind, we shouldered our poles and carried them into the stadium.

It was cloudy, warm, and humid, with gusty winds from the south. Devils or no devils, it was a good day for pole vaulting.

I remembered what Grandma said to me. She doesn't believe in the devil. She says, "There is only one presence in my life and in the universe, God the good, and that's all there is."

I felt all that goodness filling me with energy as I warmed up for the biggest track meet of my life. I stepped in line behind the other vaulters and said, "Good afternoon! Isn't this a beautiful day for vaulting?"

The two girls in front of me jerked their heads around. They looked nervous and frightened, so I smiled at them.

Alex said, "Good afternoon, Maggie!"

"Hey there!" I said.

The girl in front of me thought I was talking to her, so I pretended that I was. "Good to see you!" I said, nodding at her.

"You can't see me, silly," Alex said. "But it's good to see you! This runway will be nice and fast, and with this tailwind, you should be able to hold pretty high."

"Great! I'm so looking forward to it!"

The girl in front of me looked confused, and then ran down the runway. I turned around to see who'd lined up behind me. It was You Know Who, from St. Bishop.

"Hey, Amanda! How are you?" I said, honestly happy to see her.

Amanda flashed her fashion-model smile. "Hey! It's Maggie, right?"

I nodded, flattered that she remembered me.

"I see you finally got a real pole," she said.

I laughed. "My other one broke. I've had this about two weeks. It works really well."

"Good luck!" she said. And I think she really meant it. "You too. How many events are you in?"

"The pole vault, hurdles, 100, and the 4-by-100 relay."

"Well, I'm sure you'll win them all," I said.

Amanda looked at me hard, to see if I was making fun of her. When she saw my smiling face, she smiled back at me.

Someone had laid a long white measuring tape alongside the run-way, held down with strips of white athletic tape to keep it from blowing around. That way we could find our marks without having to measure for ourselves. I thought it was a great idea. I'd never seen it done before.

I found my starting spot and took off. With my new spikes and a tailwind, I ran faster than ever. I jumped into the plant and felt the pole bend. When it unbent, I zoomed straight up the pole. There was no crossbar, but I'm sure I was as high as I'd ever been in my life.

"Perfect!" Alex said. "You're ready. No sense wearing yourself out. The starting height is nine feet, but I think you should pass until ten."

"I can do that."

"Do what?" Scott asked.

"I'm going to start at ten feet."

I looked to see Amanda waiting on the runway. She'd just watched me go almost as high as she had when we'd last competed. She had a strange look on her face. Was it fear?

She ran down and planted her pole, but she was way under on her step. She stalled out and landed on the right side of the pit, then jumped onto the running track. I put my foot where she'd taken off from. She seemed flustered as she stepped to check her mark.

"Way under," she said. "This pole is pretty soft. I might have to use one of my stiffer poles and move my step back with this tailwind."

"How many poles do you have?" I asked.

"Only three right now," she said. "But I've got another one coming for the state meet."

I went over and sat down next to Scott. "Do you know what she has?" I asked.

Scott stared at Amanda. She looked stunning in her dark blue warm-ups. "I'm about to find out," he said, referring to her skimpy uniform.

"Hello?" I said. "She's got three poles and a fourth on the way."

"That's nice," Scott said, not hearing a word I'd said.

I looked around for my parents, but they weren't here yet.

"Okay! Lady pole-vaulters!" the official said. "Please come over for final instructions!"

The official was the first woman pole vault official I'd seen. She was wearing a white polo shirt with a KSHSAA emblem, which Scott told me stood for Kansas State High School Activities Association. She was about the same age as Miss Jamison, but very serious. An official official.

"Welcome to the regional meet," she said. "We'll be running this event according to the rules, so you'll have ninety seconds to vault after your name is called. The starting height is nine feet. Are there any passes? If so, give me your name and the height you want to start at." She raised her pencil to her clipboard.

I raised my hand. So did Amanda, and a few other girls.

"So we have ten vaulters, and five of you are starting at the opening height," the official said. "Let's begin."

Two boys wearing red Erie Red Devil football t-shirts stood on either side of the pit. "Put the bar at nine feet!" the official shouted at them.

I went over and put my running flats back on. Then I had to wait about forty-five minutes for the bar to get up to ten feet. I finally started warming up when it got to nine-six. I did about half the drills I usually do, including full sprints, in my new spikes.

"The bar is going to ten feet! Steele is up! The clock is running!"

Suddenly my heart was racing. I felt a strong gust of wind at my back and took off down the runway. My plant was perfect. When the pole unbent, I shot way over the bar.

"Whew! That was nerve-racking," I said, sitting down.

Scott held his hands about two feet apart and said, "But you made it by that much. You were flying!"

Only one girl went out at ten feet, which left six of us still in. I made ten-six on my first attempt, just as easily as I'd made ten feet. Amanda made it on her first attempt too, but not by much. She was still way under on her step, but she used her athletic ability to make it over the bar.

"She looks great, doesn't she?" Scott said, watching her walk over to the stands to talk to her parents. They weren't smiling.

At eleven feet, the official said, "There are five vaulters left in the competition. The order is as follows: Dixon up, Cooper on deck, Steele on hold, McCurdy and Cunningham, be ready!"

Dixon and Cooper missed their first attempts at eleven feet.

"Steele, you're up! The clock is running!" The official was good at keeping the competition going, but she wasn't friendly like Mr. Bright. I felt all jumpy and nervous.

I picked up my pole and went to my spot on the runway. I looked to see if my parents had shown up. They'd missed my first two jumps and were almost an hour late.

I heard someone shout, "Go, Maggie!" from the stands way over on the other side of the football field. Mr. Bright was waving at me with both arms. Mom and Dad and Grandma stood next to him. There they were! I smiled.

"Maggie!" Alex shouted. "You've got thirty seconds to vault!"

I felt a jolt of panic. I took a moment to imagine myself going over the bar. But the official stepped onto the runway, waving a red flag on a stick.

"Time!" she shouted. "Steele, that's a miss!"

Scott shook his head as I sat down. "What happened to you? You just stood there talking to yourself. Are you all right? Don't let the pressure get to you now!"

Amanda ran down the runway in her skimpy top and bikini shorts. She soared over the bar by a foot, no problem. I swallowed hard. As the first vaulter to clear eleven feet, she'd taken the lead in the competition. Cunningham also made it on her first attempt.

"Second attempt at eleven feet, Dixon, Cooper, and Steele, in that order!"

Dixon brushed it with her arm but made it over. She clapped and her people cheered really loud. It must've been her best jump ever. Cooper missed badly. And then it was my turn.

I was still a nervous wreck. Being red-flagged felt like getting arrested or something. My heart was pounding. I took off running, with plenty of time left on the clock. But just as I passed my midpoint check mark, Alex shouted, "STOP! STOP! STOP!"

I slammed on my brakes. "What!?" I shouted. I must have looked like a lunatic.

"You were way ahead of your mid-mark! You would've been too far under. If you're going to run that hard at the beginning, move your step back a foot."

"Thirty seconds!" The official shouted. I ran back to my mark, checked the measuring tape, and moved my step back.

"Go! Now!" Alex shouted.

I was out of breath. My heart was pounding. I took off down the runway, feeling rushed and out of control. My step was off. Everything felt wrong. I kicked the bar off and felt a sharp pain as I landed on my feet on the pad.

Crack! My right foot landed on the crossbar. I fell onto the pad and grabbed my ankle.

Coach Dillinger and Scott got there quickly. "Was that your ankle that cracked?" Scott asked.

"No, I broke the cross bar!" I shouted. "I'm okay, I'm okay!"

I stepped down off the front pad, but when I tried to stand up, a jolt of pain shot through my ankle, forcing me to sit on the ground next to the runway. The helpers quickly removed the broken crossbar away and put the spare one up on the pegs.

The official shouted, "Cunningham is up! Cooper on deck!" Then she looked down at me and raised her eyebrows. "Steele, you still have one attempt. Are you okay?"

"Yes, I'm fine. I'm okay."

Coach D took off my spike and squeezed my ankle. I jerked my leg back. "That hurts!" I shouted.

He moved it around, testing it. Everything he did hurt. Coach D unzipped the pouch around his waist and pulled out a roll of white tape. He pushed my toes up.

"Hold your foot right there," he said, and began taping my ankle.

My thoughts flashed back to the last time I'd seen him trying to fix something with white tape—my broken bamboo pole. But this time, he wasn't going to let me down.

"You should be able to run on that, for a while anyway," he said.

"Cooper up!" the official shouted. "Followed by Steele!"

I couldn't get my fat taped foot into my narrow spiked shoe. I started to panic again. Scott ran over, carrying my flats. "Here! Wear these!"

I tied them on. The taped foot fit, but it was tight.

"Steele is up! The clock is running!"

Coach Dillinger helped me to my feet. Scott handed me my pole. I jogged up the runway, testing my ankle. The tape felt tight, and my ankle hurt. But it was all right. It had to be.

I knew the clock was ticking, but for some reason I didn't feel out of control or pressed for time. I took in a big breath of Grandma's goodness and said, "Time to be brave, Maggie," before letting it out again.

"You can do it, Sis!" Alex said. "Just like in the barn!"

Pushed from behind by a gusty southern tailwind, I lifted my florescent green vaulting pole and started down the runway, toward the planting box and the landing pad and the yellow crossbar, towering eleven feet high in the troubled Kansas sky.

Seven...six...five...

Counting backward with each left footstep, I sprinted faster and faster, my brown braid bouncing with each stride.

Getting over the crossbar would mean at least fourth place, which was a really big deal because the top four finishers qualify for the state meet in Wichita, and I'd never been to state in anything, except to show sheep at the Kansas State Fair.

But now, since I'd already missed twice at this height, this was my last chance, do or die. Make it, and I was going to state. Miss it, and I was going back to the farm, maybe for the rest of my life.

Four... three...two...

Powering along as fast as I could, I raised my hands high above my head, and—*one!*

I jammed the pole into the box, jumped left-footed into the takeoff, and held on tight, bending my knees toward my chest and waiting for the ride of my life.

The pole curved away to my left like a long green ribbon. When the pole sprang back, I was launched like a rocket into total weightlessness, which is the most awesome feeling I've ever experienced, and then there was the crossbar, with my future riding on it...

After everything we'd been through, this would either be the very best vault, or the very last vault, of my life. But from the first step down the runway, I knew I was going to make it.

I'll never forget the sight of that yellow crossbar, hanging up there in the cloudy sky.

Coach Dillinger helped me out of the pit.

"That was one of the bravest things I've ever seen," he said.

The official smiled. "That puts you in at least fourth place," she said. "Would you like to keep vaulting, or are you done for the day?" She pointed at my ankle with her clipboard.

"Oh, that," I said. "To tell you the truth, I didn't feel a thing!"

The official turned and said, "Move the bar to eleven-six!"

"It's just a strain at this point," Coach said. "I'm going to stop you now so you'll be able to jump next week in Wichita."

To tell the truth, my ankle had stiffened up quite a bit. I wasn't sure I could run fast enough to make eleven-six in my flats. "Okay, that's enough for today," I said.

"The bar is at eleven-six," the official announced. "We have three contestants remaining. One contestant has withdrawn, in fourth place!" She turned to me. "Congratulations, Miss Steele. That was impressive. Good luck at state!"

State! That had a nice ring to it!

"Let's get you over to the bleachers and get some ice on that ankle," Coach said. "Scott, give me a hand and we'll help her across the field."

Just then a booming voice said, "Step away from my girlfriend!"

Troy reached down and picked me up like I weighed nothing. I grabbed him around the neck. "Way to go, Maggie!" he said, kissing me in front of everybody. "I saw the whole thing from over there." He tilted his head toward the shot put ring.

"How'd you do?"

"Personal best, fifty-four feet. And I won!"

"Looks like we're both going to Wichita to state," I said. "You can carry me all the way there if you want."

"Maggie, I'd carry you anywhere."

"I bet you say that to all your pole-vaulting girlfriends!" I said, and kissed him back.

CHAPTER 43

My parents and Grandma and Mr. Bright were standing and cheering as Troy carried me across the track and set me down over the railing. Coach Dillinger took a funny-looking plastic thingy and cut the tape off my ankle, which was purple and swollen, then filled a plastic bag with ice and put it on my ankle, which was propped up on big Troy's leg.

"Wow! Man alive, that's cold!"

"Ten minutes, no more," Coach said, all businesslike.

"How about less? A lot less!" I said. Everybody laughed, even the coach.

The icy pain turned into cold numbness, reminding me of when I'd used Alex's ice pack last summer, after running away. People came up to congratulate me, and I was nodding and saying thanks, but my mind was on how everything had turned out since then.

"Thank you. Thank you. Thank you." People thought I was thanking them, but I was really thanking my brother.

I heard him whisper, "No, thank you, Sis. You were amazing down there this afternoon. But we're not finished yet!"

"Oh, yes, I'm finished!" I hollered. "Get this thing off of me before I freeze to death!"

Troy unwrapped the ice bag, dried my ankle with a towel, and rewrapped my ankle with an elastic bandage. My future doctor seemed like an expert.

"You do good work, Dr. Timmerman," I said. Troy took one of his own clean socks from his athletic bag and put it on my foot. It went clear up over my knee.

Grandma cackled. "Looks like a sock on a rooster!"

I hopped over to her and gave her a big hug.

"That was a very brave thing you did," she said. "But I have one question."

"What's that?" I said quickly, sitting down next to her.

"Looks to me like you're always talking to somebody before you jump."

"What?"

She whispered into my ear, "How long have you been talking to your brother?"

My mind went as numb as my ankle. I opened my mouth to say something, but Grandma held me close.

"Don't worry," she continued. "I won't tell. Your secret is safe with me. I've been talking with my husband for thirty-five years."

Across the field, Amanda McCurdy was curving over the crossbar, the winner at twelve feet. She was amazing, pure and simple.

Grandma squeezed my arm. "I'm so glad they let you pole-vault with your clothes on."

"Me too! I love you, Grandma," I said, hugging her. At last, somebody else knew my big secret. Of course it would have to be Grandma, who else?

It was all good!

CHAPTER 44

As the only two state qualifiers from Grain Valley, Troy and I rode to Wichita in the school van with Coach Dillinger and his wife. It was like being in a dream, riding to the state finals with my boyfriend, holding hands and watching the sunrise over the beautiful Flint Hills.

Coach Dillinger talked nonstop most of the way to Wichita about the Kansas State High School Track and Field Championships. He waved his hands a lot. It was funny to hear his wife shout, "Edward! Keep your hands on the wheel!" because we'd never heard anyone get on Coach D's case like that about anything.

Anyway, the drive to Wichita was wonderful. Did I mention that Troy and I held hands all of the way there?

"There are lots of big high school track meets," Coach D said, "but this is the biggest in the entire nation, with over three thousand participants. Takes two whole days to run it. It's been held for one hundred years; in fact, this will be year one hundred and one. It's a big accomplishment just to get here. The important thing for you two is to do your best and have fun."

Troy squeezed my hand. We were already having fun.

"A lot of athletes have lifetime best performances at this meet because it's so inspirational," Coach continued. "I saw a high jumper once, from a little tiny school. He'd never jumped higher than six-six in his entire life. But he jumped seven-one that day at the state meet because there were about twenty thousand people to cheer him over the bar."

I couldn't imagine what it would feel like to pole-vault in front of twenty thousand people, but I was about to find out.

Coach was still talking. "Cessna Stadium has been the site of many historic track and field moments. The greatest high school miler ever, Jim Ryun, who went to Wichita East back in the sixties, ran some of his best races on that track, which of course was a cinder track back then. Then, in the seventies, the USTFF and USATF National Championships were held at Cessna Stadium. The best runners and throwers and jumpers in the nation—we're talking world-class Olympians—came to Wichita, and I saw them all."

He looked in the rearview mirror. "Troy, you'll be throwing in the same ring as the great shot-putters, like Al Feuerbach, one of the best in the world. Guess where he went to college?"

"I don't know, K State?" Troy guessed.

"Nope! Emporia State! Can you believe that? And Maggie, Earl Bell set a world record at Cessna Stadium in 1976. I saw it myself. Eighteen feet, seven inches!"

"That's the same guy who sent me my new pole! Right?"

"Yep, Earl picked it out just for you. I'd say he knows a thing or two about picking poles, don't you think?"

I nodded, wondering where I'd be without Mr. Bright and Earl Bell, and my new pole. Certainly I wouldn't be in this van, going to state.

"How's your ankle feeling by now?" Coach asked.

I rolled my foot around and around. "I think I'm good to go," I said, smiling at him.

"Good to know!" he said. "I'm sure you'll do great in the big show!"

CHAPTER 45

As the van rolled into Wichita on the northeast side of town, I imagined three thousand other athletes like us, coming from all over Kansas to compete. It gave me goose bumps.

"Good luck," I said, squeezing Troy's hand.

"You too," he said. "Have fun!"

The light poles of Cessna Stadium, on the campus of Wichita State University, were the highest landmarks on this side of the city, and the stadium itself was by far the biggest I'd ever seen. The bleachers went way, way, up, and the press box went even higher. It was so tall that by the time Coach parked in the lot at 9:45, we couldn't see the top of it from inside the van.

According to the schedule, the Class 3A girls' pole vault and 3A boys' shot put were both scheduled for 11:30. Coach D left us to unload while he went to the coaches' check-in. He came back carrying a packet with our numbers in them. My number was 373. Troy showed me how to fasten it to my uniform top with safety pins, below the GV.

"Do we get to keep these?" I asked.

"Yep, it's yours," Troy said. "You can buy yourself a state meet t-shirt, too. Everybody does."

I was excited about taking home a souvenir from the state track meet. Troy and I carried our stuff through the gate underneath the west side of the stadium and walked up the concrete ramp that led up to the bleachers. When we got to the opening, there was so much to see, I couldn't take it all in at first. Across the field a hundred or more brightly colored team tents were set up high in the stadium. Thousands of spectators were packed into the rows below.

The running track itself was a sight to behold. The long pole vault runway ran the length of the east side of the field, across from us. There were landing pads and standards set up in two locations, one in the middle, and one on the north end.

"Two pits?" I asked, astonished.

Troy nodded. "Impressive, isn't it?"

It was, in fact, the coolest place I'd ever seen. In addition to the awesome facility, the weather was perfect. The sky was bright blue, with a few high white clouds. The forecast we'd heard in the van said there'd be a high of eighty-five degrees, with south winds gusting fifteen to twenty miles per hour.

Was I really about to compete in the state championship meet in front of twenty thousand people on an absolutely perfect day for pole vaulting?

"Is this like heaven or what?" I asked Alex.

"I can tell you it looks like heaven to me," Alex whispered.

Troy helped me carry my pole to the middle pit, which was where my event was to be held. He gave me a hug and jogged off to get his shot put weighed in. I started warming up around the infield, taking it all in.

It was so exciting to be here, with the crowd and the other state qualifiers, athletes who looked so fit and capable. The man's voice on the public address system echoed through the giant stadium, making everything sound super exciting.

There were volunteers and officials all over the place, and everything seemed so well organized. They set up the yellow hurdles really fast, and after the races were over they got them off just as fast. I was really impressed.

I noticed there was a sign painted on a building at the end of the track: "Shocker Track and Field, a Championship Tradition." It listed all the championships WSU's track teams had won, and there were a lot of them.

The announcer said, "First call, girls' 3A pole vault. Competing in the 3A pole vault will be..." He read off all of the entries, including Amanda McCurdy from St. Bishop, and—wait for it—"Maggie Steele of Grain Valley!"

I felt a jolt go through me. Sure, he'd called out fifteen other names, but it was amazing to hear my name echo through such a ginormous stadium. I jogged back to my stuff and was stretching when Alex said, "Welcome to the Midwest's premier high school track and field carnival!"

"Carnival? I thought this was a track meet."

"They call the big track meets carnivals because they're like a three-ring circus, with so many things going on at the same time."

The announcer said, "Second call, 3A pole vault."

I laughed. "He does sound like a ringmaster, doesn't he?"

"It's the Greatest Show on Earth, Maggie, and you're in the center ring! But this will be the hottest day of the season, and the runway temperature will be ten to fifteen degrees hotter. So be sure to drink plenty of liquids, okay?"

"Okay, Coach Alex!" I said. I pulled a plastic bottle of grape PowerAde from my bag and took a big drink.

It took a long time for sixteen pole-vaulters to get their steps marked on a new runway. Then the head official called us together. He was an older man with wire-rimmed glasses and a bright smile.

"Welcome to the state meet, and congratulations on just being here," he said. "All of you know the rules; they're the same as regionals. When your name is called, the stopwatch will start, and you will have ninety seconds to take your vault."

The other official was the same woman from the Erie regional. She would be holding the stop watch and the red flag. Suddenly I felt anxious about being on the clock again.

The head official continued, "We'll start at nine feet and go up six inches at a time. Now, if you pass three heights in a row, you can take a run-through without the bar. When I call your name, let me know where you want to start. Any questions?"

The girl from Bluestem raised her hand.

"Yes?"

"I heard the wind swirls around really bad down here," she said. "Like sometimes you'll think it's a tailwind, but it's really a crosswind or even a headwind. So can we have someone near the takeoff let us know which way the wind is blowing? Is that legal?"

The official tapped his pencil on the clipboard and pointed to the sign board on the infield, near the pit. "See that ribbon hanging over there?" There was a long Day-Glo orange ribbon blowing in the wind. "That will give you some idea which way the wind is blowing down here. But let me say this: I've officiated this event for ten years, and the most successful vaulters don't worry about the wind. Fact is, you won't have time to wait for the wind to shift when you are on the clock, so I strongly suggest that you focus on what you can control. Okay? That's my word to the wise this morning. Any other questions?"

Nobody had any. I didn't know what to think about what the girl from Bluestem had said. I told the official that I'd start at ten feet. Several other girls were starting at nine-six. Amanda McCurdy passed until ten-six. In addition to pole-vaulting, she was also running the 100, 4-by-100 relay, and hurdling. She was going to have a very busy day.

We stood in line on the runway, waiting for our final run-throughs. "Good luck, Amanda," I said.

"Thanks, Maggie," Amanda said. "Hey, how's your ankle?"

I hadn't thought about it since testing it in the van.

"Totally good, thanks for asking." I gestured to the stadium around us. "This feels like a great place to vault!"

Amanda shook her head. "That girl from Bluestem knows what she's talking about. There are bad crosswinds in this place."

I followed Amanda's eyes to the ribbon tied to the sign board. The ribbon flapped wildly, showing a crosswind from the west, then dropped straight down, then showed a tailwind from the south, all in less than thirty seconds.

"Why's it doing that?" I asked.

Amanda turned and pointed behind us. Looking toward the south end of the stadium, I could see a tall building with a clock tower on the hill in the distance. The clock face looked like the grandfather clock in our living room. The time was 11:15. An American flag on top of the clock tower was flapping wildly.

"See how it's blowing hard from the south up there?" Amanda asked. "Well, by the time it gets down here, it's different. The wind gets caught and swirls, because we're below ground level, in a bowl."

When it was Amanda's turn to take her second warm-up vault, the woman official blocked the runway and motioned her aside. She pointed at Amanda's bare belly, shook her head, and said something I couldn't hear. Amanda raised her waxed eyebrows and slumped her shoulders.

"What's going on?" I whispered.

"Looks like the fashion police have put an end to the Amanda McCurdy show," Alex said.

"But why?"

"Apparently it's against the rules for such a beautiful athlete to compete here with so much perfect skin showing."

Amanda stomped over to her stuff and pulled her full-length team uniform out of her bag. Her hands trembled as she unpinned the number from her half tank top and pinned it to the shirt. She pulled out a pair of team shorts and put them on over her bikini bottoms before taking her place at the back of the warm-up line.

"I suppose it's a public safety issue," Alex said.

"How's that?"

"Well, just imagine all the heart attacks and strokes she's prevented by putting her clothes back on."

"That's terrible," I said.

"But it's true. So true."

Several girls, including Amanda, had trouble getting off the ground during warm-ups because they were bothered by the crosswind. When it was my turn, Alex said, "No matter what might be going on with these other vaulters, you can't worry about the wind. You've got great speed, and this is the fastest runway you've ever had. So focus on that, okay?"

"Okay!"

I was totally ready. After all, my ankle wasn't swollen. I'd been able to put my spikes on, no problem. And I had an awesome new pole. I forgot all about looking to see which way the ribbon was blowing. I just took off down the runway.

The surface felt springy and fast. I planted with lots of power and held my position as the pole bent. I tucked my knees into my chest and thrust my hips up at just the right moment, extending my feet to the sky, and the pole shot me straight in the air. Man alive, I was flying!

"You're good to go!" Alex said. "No more warm-ups! Get a big drink. Take your spikes off. Put on your flats and drink the rest of your sports drink."

"But I don't want to go sloshing down the runway, do I?"

Alex laughed. "Think about it. It's going to be hot down here. You need to keep from dehydrating. A lot of these girls won't drink nearly enough liquids today. You should also eat something now, to keep your strength. Have a bite of banana, maybe a few almonds."

I was too excited to even think about food. "But I'm not hungry."

"Doesn't matter. This competition may last two hours or more. You haven't eaten since breakfast, and it's almost lunchtime."

It was exactly 11:30 but there were still several girls on the runway. Amanda tried to sweet-talk the official into letting her take a third run-through. The woman official looked up at the big clock and shook her head. Amanda's cover-girl smile vanished. She found her parents in the stands and raised her arms in a "what gives?" gesture. They stood up, looking concerned. Amanda stomped over to her stuff and threw her pole down. The official hadn't seen her temper tantrum, which I figured was a good thing for Amanda.

"And so the drama begins!" Alex said. "Welcome to the center ring!"

CHAPTER 46

As I waited my turn to vault, I ate some of my banana and a handful of salted almonds. Alex was right, I was hungry. I also ate a few bites of energy bar, and washed it all down with some more PowerAde. I felt nature calling. I went to the head official to let him know I was going to the restroom.

"Okay, you're passing to ten feet. You have plenty of time," he said.

I ducked under a string of black and yellow flags, crossed over the track, and climbed up into the stadium bleachers. Then I heard some-one shout, "Maggie Steele!" Mr. Bright was standing and waving. I was walking up the concrete steps toward the ramp that went down under the stadium, and he motioned for me to meet him there.

It was shady and cool under the stadium. The smell of popcorn and hot dogs from the concession stand told me that I needed to finish my snacks when I got back down to the field. Mr. Bright was wearing a Grain Valley shirt, a matching hat, and a big smile. I was happy to see him. As he gestured I could see the scars on his hands.

"Your warm-up vault was perfect!" he said. "Good idea to stop with one. No sense wearing yourself out in this heat. What a great day to vault!"

"Thanks for everything," I said. "I wouldn't be here if you hadn't bought the pole for me. I'm glad you're here to see me use it."

Mr. Bright got really choked up at that point. His face had a lot of pain in it. He placed his hands on top of mine.

"You'll never know how much it means to see you down there," he said. "If your brother could be here, and Caleb—why, I can't imagine how thrilled they'd be..."

He shook my hands for emphasis, his face pinched with emotion.

"You go down there and give it all you've got, and that will be good enough. You're ready to put it all together, I can see it. We'll be right up there, cheering for you!"

I hugged Mr. Bright and kissed him on the cheek. When I got back down to the infield, I ate the rest of my banana and some more almonds and then searched up in the stands, because Mom and Dad and Grandma were up there, somewhere. I finally saw someone I recognized, but it wasn't my folks. It was Zack-a-roo. He was sitting on his dad's shoulders, waving a big sign that read *Go Maggie Go!*

I stood up and waved. People stood up next to them. I recognized so many who had supported me. Along with the Wilsons were the woman from the school board and her daughter, Holly, and—oh, there they were! Mom and Dad and Grandma. She was sitting under a blue umbrella to keep out of the sun. I waved at everybody and they all waved back. I got a lump in my throat, thinking how they'd come all the way to Wichita to watch me.

"You've made a lot of people happy, Maggie," Alex said. "They feel part of your success, and they believe in you. I'm absolutely certain this will be a day they'll never forget."

I nodded, feeling a bit overwhelmed.

"When the bar gets to nine-six, you should go through half of your warm-up again. You'll want to be sweaty and fired up when it's your turn."

"Sweaty?" I laughed.

"Sweaty, perspiring, glowing, whatever. Just make sure you're ready to run fast, okay?"

When the bar got to nine-six, I spent fifteen minutes or so jogging and stretching, skipping and then all-out sprinting, and counting my left footsteps backward, jumping up and pretending to plant an imaginary pole. I was absolutely ready to rock and roll.

It was 12:10 when the bar finally reached ten feet. Only two vaulters had been eliminated. Alex was right, this was going to be a long competition. When my name was finally called, Alex met me on the runway as usual. But what he said next gave me a real jolt.

"I want you to pretend like they just changed the rules. Today you get one, and only one, attempt at each height. That means no misses!"

I nodded, because it made perfect sense. Today was the day to make every vault count, like it was my only chance. The clock was ticking, but instead of feeling anxious, like I had at regionals, I felt like a rocket on a launching pad, ready for the countdown. I saw a perfect vault in my head, took a deep breath, and ran down the runway.

My legs felt powerful and strong, and I ran really fast. I planted the pole just as perfectly as I had in warm-ups, and when the pole unbent, I was so far over ten feet, it was ridiculous.

I walked past the woman official. She gave me a big smile. "Nice start!" she said.

"Thanks!" I could sense that she really wanted me to jump well. I went over and sat down.

"You made a huge statement with that vault," Alex said. "Everyone saw you clear that by at least two feet. Now I think it's time for a little gamesmanship."

"What?" I asked.

"Let's wait until he calls your name for ten-six, and then I want you to shout, in your most confident voice, that you're passing to eleven."

"Okay, but, can I do that? Pass twice in the same meet?"

"Yes, you can, and today you should. Now put your flats back on and go under the stadium for about ten minutes or so, to get out of this blazing sun."

I went to the restroom and splashed some cold water on my face. It was nice and cool. My mind was still on pole-vaulting, but my body was relaxing. When I went back down and sat next to my stuff, Amanda jogged by, warming up for her first attempt at ten-six.

"Great vault," she said, stopping to stretch. Her smile seemed forced. She really looked stressed.

I figured she was under a lot of pressure, with so many events and everyone expecting her to win them all.

"You doing okay?" I asked.

"The vault coach from KU is sitting with my parents," she said, point-ing up into the stands. The KU coach wore a blue shirt with a Jayhawk on the pocket. He had a pen in his hand and a clipboard on his knee. I felt like he was watching us.

"I've been going to his vault camp since I was like twelve," Amanda said. "He's ready to offer me a scholarship if I jump well today, but I'm not sure KU is where I want to go."

"Why not?"

"Well, because both of my parents ran track at KU, and I'm not sure I could ever do as well as they did, you know?"

I nodded, but I didn't know. My folks knew next to nothing about track and field. I couldn't imagine how Amanda felt. Maybe like she was under a microscope.

Just then the official shouted, "The bar is going up to ten-six. There are five vaulters left. Steele! First attempt!"

I stood up and shouted, "Steele passes to eleven feet!"

"Steele passes to eleven feet," he said, nodding as he marked the clipboard.

Amanda's eyes got wide. I grinned and continued our little conversation. "You've got time to figure out what you want to do. So why not enjoy this? We're vaulting at one of the very best places to vault in the whole world."

Amanda smirked. "Who told you that?"

"Don't you know? Earl Bell set a world record right here. What's keeping us from doing our best here, too?"

Amanda smiled at me like I was her only friend. "Thanks a lot, Maggie," she said sincerely.

I watched her select one of her poles and take off down the runway. She made ten-six by a mile, and then looked up to her parents in the stands. But her parents were already reviewing her vault on the video camera, with the KU coach looking over their shoulder. They were too busy to notice their daughter.

"That sucks," I muttered.

"It sure does," Alex said. "She's one of the most beautiful young women on the planet, and I'm unable to ask her out!"

"Funny."

"You said exactly what she needed to hear. She's feeling so much pressure, she can't enjoy what she's doing, just for the sake of doing it. You're a good sport, Sis."

I felt glad I wasn't being watched by a college recruiter, or video-taped by track-expert parents. All I was thinking about was doing my best, and having fun.

Of the five remaining vaulters, three missed their first attempts at ten-six, including the girl from Bluestem. She wasted more than a minute on the runway, watching the wind ribbon, then she stopped halfway down the runway because, I guess, she felt a gust of wind in her face. By the time she got back to her mark, the woman official was waving the red flag at her. I knew what that felt like.

"She's really freaked out," I said.

"Yep, it's unfortunate," Alex agreed.

"But that's not me, not today."

"That's right, Sis. Time to get some more liquid in you. Eat a few more bites of energy bar. Time to start your engine for eleven feet!"

The girl from Bluestem also missed her final attempt. What she had feared had come to pass. But the girl from Sabetha made ten-six on her third attempt.

The official called out, "Eleven feet!" and at the same instant, the PA announcer said, "In the girls' 3A pole vault, the bar is being raised to eleven feet. There are four jumpers left in the competition."

I felt a burst of excitement, realizing that I was one of them.

"Steele up! The clock is running!"

"You don't need any more coaching from me, Sis," Alex said. "Time to rock! Make this one count!"

I went to my mark, took a deep breath, and ran down the runway. My second vault of the day felt even better than the first. When I got up there, the crossbar was far below me. As I bounded from the pit I heard the Grain Valley folks cheering for me. I looked up in the stands. There was Zack, jumping up and down and shaking his *Go Maggie Go!* sign.

I sat down to catch my breath.

"You keep vaulting like that, and I'll have to alert Mission Control," Alex said.

"Why's that?"

"To prepare for your lunar landing!"

I took a long drink from my second bottle of grape PowerAde. I looked up at the clock. It was 1:15. A whole hour had passed, but it felt like maybe twenty minutes.

Amanda made eleven feet on her first try, but the girls from Wichita Collegiate and Sabetha both missed. When the Collegiate vaulter made it on her second try, the announcer was really excited about it. "That's Tara Lynn Smithson from Wichita Collegiate over the bar at eleven feet! Amanda McCurdy from St. Bishop and Maggie Steele from Grain Valley are also over this height. Leslie Bunker of Sabetha has one attempt remaining at eleven feet."

The people in the Grain Valley cheering section went crazy when my name was announced. This was getting a little embarrassing, but I smiled and waved anyway.

Since there were no races going on at that moment, every eye in the stadium was on the poor girl from Sabetha. I couldn't imagine how it felt to be singled out like that. Someone started clapping. Clap! Clap! Clap! Other people clapped too. But by the time she got down the runway, the clapping was all out of rhythm, she missed badly, and her state meet was history.

"The bar will be going to eleven-six with three contestants left. Steele is up, McCurdy on deck, Smithson on hold. Steele, the clock is running!"

Alex was super excited. "Okay, Sis, first attempt! Make it count! Here we go now, here we go!"

I didn't need to think about what to do. The vault felt perfect, like it was happening in slow motion. It took a long time to hit the landing pad.

"That's Maggie Steele of Grain Valley, the first 3A vaulter over eleven feet, six inches this afternoon!"

I'd just vaulted higher than I'd ever jumped, but I wasn't even out of breath. Alex said something, but I didn't hear it.

"What?"

"I said sit down and get a drink!"

I took a drink of my PowerAde. It was warm, but at least it was wet.

Alex's voice was calmer now. "Pay attention to this moment. Remember what that felt like, because you're going to do it all over again in about ten minutes."

Amanda made her first attempt at eleven-six, but not by much. She gave me a funny look as she walked by. I nodded and smiled, but my focus was elsewhere.

Smithson's supporters tried the clap-clap thing for her, too, but it was pretty lame. She missed badly, like she didn't believe she could really make it. Since Amanda and I had already made eleven-six, the official gave Smithson a couple of minutes' rest before her second attempt, which she missed, and then more time before her third, but she missed again on her last try.

"Twelve feet!" the official shouted.

The announcer said, "In the 3A girls' pole vault, the bar is going up to twelve feet. Steele of Grain Valley and McCurdy of St. Bishop are the only two vaulters left in the competition."

I heard the announcer call my name, but this time it sounded like a voice in the far-off distance. I went to the runway and stood at my mark.

"Okay, Maggie!" Alex said. "Now's the time!"

I felt the same wonderful feeling all over again, and over I went.

"That's Maggie Steele of Grain Valley, over the bar at twelve feet!"

I went over, sat down, and got another drink. My heart was pounding but my mind stayed right where it was, focused on that feeling. Amanda missed her first attempt at twelve feet, but not by much. She made it on her second try, brushing the bar with her arm. It was still bouncing up there as she stepped off the landing pad.

"That's Amanda McCurdy of St. Bishop over at twelve feet!" the announcer said.

"Twelve-six!" the official shouted.

The announcer said, "In the class 3A girls' pole vault, the bar will be raised to twelve feet six inches. This, ladies and gentlemen, would be a new all-time, all-class state meet record!"

The stadium crowd responded with a big cheer.

I stood on my mark on the runway.

Alex was shouting to be heard. "Suck in your stomach when you get up there over the bar. See you on the other side! Don't forget to wave to the crowd!"

They say time stands still in the most memorable moments of our lives. That a flashbulb goes off somewhere in our brains, capturing the images forever. Like the pictures on the mantel in our living room. The one of my brother with his girlfriend, as happy as they'd ever be, and the one next to it, showing me stiff-arming a guy who will never, ever get to kiss me.

Other snapshots fill the photo album in my mind. A man with scarred hands, clapping and stomping his feet. My parents, hugging each other tight. A little boy, waving a sign with my name on it. Grandma beaming under her parasol, as her faith became sight.

Twenty thousand people took home their own images of the vault I made that day. Someone took a photo of me standing on the landing pad, beneath the towering crossbar, waving to the cheering crowd. They mailed it to us. It's on the mantel, too.

The photo proves I really did it.

I was over the moon.

Chapter 47

Up in the stadium bleachers, two men wearing black shirts and big smiles waited patiently as my fan club hugged me and pounded me on the back. One of the men was tall and had a completely shaved head. The other was shorter and wore a black cap with *Shockers Track & Field* written in gold. Kangaroo Zack jumped into my arms and wouldn't let go, so I held him on my hip and extended my hand to meet them.

"My name is Steve Rainbolt," the tall man said. "I'm the head track coach here at Wichita State, and we just wanted to say congratulations! This is my pole vault coach, Pat Wilson."

"Nice to meet you," I said.

"You are the most technically advanced high school vaulter I've ever seen," Coach Wilson said.

"Really?!"

"Who's your coach?"

"Her coach is out of this world!" Grandma said.

I shot her a look that said, *Not here! Not now!*

"Well, um, I kinda, sorta just listen to the voice in my head," I said.

"But you vault so well! What camps did you attend?" Coach Rainbolt asked.

"To be honest, I taught myself at home, on the farm, up in my barn."

The coaches glanced at each other, puzzled. Then Coach Rainbolt smiled. "Well, your performance today was tremendous," he said. "Have you thought about where you're going to college?"

"We've had some really good pole-vaulters here," Coach Wilson added. "I think you could be one of the great ones."

"That's right," Coach Rainbolt said. "We'd be happy to offer you a scholarship to vault for WSU next season."

Grandma cackled. "Let me get this straight. You want our Grain Valley Thresher to become a Wichita State Wheat Shocker?" she asked.

"We do!" the coaches said at the same time.

My fan club cheered.

"Have you given any thought about what you'd like to do for your career?" Coach Rainbolt continued.

"Well, I've thought about going into teaching," I said. "And I think I'd like to be a pole vault coach, if that's a career."

"You could teach me to pole-vault!" Zack said.

"Me, too!" said Holly.

"Maybe you could come back and teach pole-vault lessons in the barn," Grandma said.

"Maybe someday," I said. "But I'd really like to go to college first."

"Well, WSU has a great education program," Coach Rainbolt said. "And if you really want to coach track and field, I can teach you."

"That sounds great, but it's really up to my mom and dad," I said.

Dad shook his head. "No, Maggie, it's not up to us," he said. "You can stay on the farm, or you can go to college, but the choice is totally up to you."

Suddenly my whole world turned around.

"But I thought you wanted me to take Alex's place. To keep the farm going. Don't you need me to stay?"

"Heavens, no!" Mom said. "If you thought that's what we wanted, you've been under the wrong impression. In fact, nothing could be further from the truth."

"That's right," Dad said.

"But what are you going to do with the farm?" I asked.

"Your father has been approached by Steadmans, who want to lease our ground starting next year," Mom said. Always looking for more and more land to till, Steadmans was the biggest corporate farming operation in the county.

Dad shrugged. "I can work some cattle and let the big boys handle the rest of it," he said. "We'll stay put in the houses and they'll lease the farm land. The property will stay in our name until—well, until whatever comes next. But you don't have to worry about it. We never intended for you to fret."

Grandma hugged me tight. "Looks like your harvest has been waiting for you right here all along," she said.

"I want you to come over to the track office to see our championship trophies," Coach Rainbolt said, "but first you need to get down there and get your gold medal!"

The medal ceremony was like being crowned Homecoming Queen of the Super Bowl or something. The announcer made a really big deal out of it because I'd vaulted higher than any other high school girl in Kansas state meet history. The stadium crowd stood and clapped for a long time. Amanda McCurdy seemed sad as she stood on the platform on the step below me, unhappy with a silver medal, which was too bad, considering what a good season she'd had. She went on to win the 100 meter hurdles and anchor the winning relay later in the day.

A woman reporter with a tape recorder interviewed me for the Wichita newspaper. She wanted to know how I'd gotten so good at pole-vaulting, but I didn't tell her the real story. While she was asking me questions, Troy grabbed me and lifted me up in the air, shouting, "Maggie Steele! State champion! All-time record holder! And my girl-friend!"

Troy couldn't leave the shot put ring during my event, but he'd watched every vault.

"You were amazing!" he said.

"How did you do?" I asked.

"Fourth place, which is good, considering I couldn't stop thinking about you."

Hand in hand, we walked across the infield to get my pole and stuff. "The track coaches here just offered me a scholarship!"

"That's great!"

"If I go here, I can still come up to see you play football in Manhat-tan."

"And I can come right here to watch you pole-vault."

"And guess what else?"

"What?" he asked as he put me down. He flashed me a perfect smile, all dimples and teeth.

"Mom and Dad don't want me to take over the farm after all! And we graduate tomorrow!"

Troy hugged me in front of twenty thousand people. "Just in time!" he said.

"Yes! Just in time!"

Coach Dillinger and his wife were waiting for us at the van. "In all my years of coming here, that was as impressive as anything I've ever seen," he said.

"Well, Coach D, it's all your fault," I said, pretending to be angry with him.

"What do you mean?" he asked.

"If you hadn't broken my pole…"

I punched him a good one on the shoulder, and we laughed and laughed.

Coach D gave us permission to ride home with my parents. But first we all went together to find Coach Rainbolt and visited the WSU track office. The number of championship trophies was really impressive. I also noticed that he had at least ten Coach of the Year awards.

"Grandma, what do you think Grandpa would have to say about all this?" I asked.

"I happen to know that your grandfather is delighted," she whispered, squeezing my hand.

On the track, the state meet was still going strong, with every athlete trying as hard as they could, and twenty thousand people cheering them on. The crowd could be heard even with our windows up and the air conditioner on as we left the crowded parking lot.

It was late afternoon, and we were on our way back home to Grain Valley. We drove back the same way we'd come, past the sprawl of Wichita, and into the open country.

I used Troy's shoulder for a pillow and nodded off, imagining what it would be like to a wear a black-and-gold uniform. I didn't wake up until we got back to the school parking lot. Troy and I hugged for a long time before he got in his truck and I got in mine. But instead of going straight home to the farm, I had someplace else to go.

By the time I got there, the sun was setting on the old cemetery.

"I can't believe today really happened," I said, laying the gold medal on Alex's headstone.

"You have the medal to prove it did," he said.

"I couldn't have done it without you, so it's your medal, too."

In the twilight, we talked about everything that happened in Wichita, and all we'd been through together. A ginormous orange moon was on rise.

"I never want to forget this," I said.

"Then why not write it all down in a book?"

"I don't think I can write a book."

"You didn't think you could pole-vault either, until you tried."

"So that means you'll help me?"

"Sure. We can get it done this summer, before you go off to college."

"You mean before *we* go to college. You're coming too, right?"

"I'll meet you on the runway, Sis, but in the meantime, you've got a story to write."

And so that's exactly what I—I mean *we*—did.

ACKNOWLEDGEMENTS

The inspiration for this story came while watching the legendary Earl Bell coach eager young vaulters at the Tailwind Pole Vaulting Club in Jamestown, Kansas. Bell, a former world record–holder and three-time Olympian, has coached the nation's top men and women vaulters, including three members of the 2012 U.S. Olympic team, Becky Holliday, Jeremy Scott, and Derek Miles. Thank you, Earl, for giving so generously of your time and expertise as the "coaching voice" in this story. Thanks also to Tailwind Coach Mark "Doc" Breault. This book would not have been possible without your support.

To the beta readers who waded through the long rough draft and came up with many great suggestions, thank you all. Special thanks to Keith and Betty Brewer, and Jim and Nancy Brewer, for your support; and to Jillian (Overstake) Forsberg, who provided details about showing sheep from her experience as a champion. Thanks also to Garrison Overstake, for your keen ear for dialogue and other helpful suggestions; and to Bethany (Overstake) Dixon, for her loving support across the miles.

Thanks also to Rev. Tim Lytle who gave Grandma the wisdom to help Maggie through the grief process. And thanks to my *Artists' Way Tribe*, for supporting my creative journey.

Finally, to my wife and best friend, Claire, who took my daily scrawls and typed them into the computer after long days of teaching. Thank you, Waz, for believing in Maggie and in me.

To those who vault, those who coach, and those who cheer them on, I'll see you all soon, over the moon.

Grant Overstake
September, 2012

ABOUT THE AUTHOR

Grant Overstake is a former *Miami Herald* Sports Writer and Kansas newspaper editor who has been writing professionally since age 18. He began his career as a part-time sports writer at *The Wichita Eagle* before attending the University of Kansas William Allen White School of Journalism, where he was awarded the national William Randolph Hearst Award, the college version of the Pulitzer Prize. Grant also competed for the KU track team; and was a USATF All-American in the decathlon. After writing sports, news, and features for *The Miami Herald*, Grant returned to his native Kansas to edit hometown newspapers, earning numerous awards. *Maggie Vaults Over the Moon* is his premier novel.

Like *Maggie* on Facebook!
Follow *Maggie* on Twitter @MaggieVaults
Visit MaggieVaultsOverTheMoon.com

EXPERIENCE 'MAGGIE' ON AUDIOBOOK!

This is a very special story, and I look forward to bringing it to listening audiences.
-- TAVIA GILBERT

The only thing better than reading *Maggie Vaults Over the Moon* is listening to the story performed by award-winning narrator Tavia Gilbert! Available now at BlackstoneAudio.com, Downpour.com, Audible.com, and other online retailers.